Aniversi

HANNAH PHIPPS

Copyright © 2013 Hannah Phipps

All rights reserved.

ISBN-13: 978-1478174745

ISBN-10: 1478174749

For Laurels.

Welcome to my invitation.

CONTENTS

PART ONE: SECTOR FOUR

Chapter 1	1
Chapter 2	15
Chapter 3	27
Chapter 4	42
Chapter 5	55
Chapter 6	69
Chapter 7	79
Chapter 8	92
Chapter 9	111

PART TWO: MT. DALORN

Chapter 10	122
Chapter 11	132

Chapter 12	144
Chapter 13	150
Chapter 14	157
Chapter 15	167

PART THREE: TERRANARY

Chapter 16	183
Chapter 17	197
Chapter 18	210
Chapter 19	218

PART FOUR: LOCHBION

Chapter 20	225

PART FIVE: THE GLASS HOTEL

Chapter 21	235
Acknowledgements	255

PART ONE: SECTOR FOUR

~~

Chapter 1

~

Emma

A chilly gust of wind blows into the icy darkness. The sun begins to rise, bringing streaks of yellows, pinks, and oranges across the dull, blank sky. Emma jolts awake as the freezing breeze slams into her face, and looks around. She knows she must get a start on the day because there is absolutely no time to lose. Her head starts throbbing from lack of sleep; she's only been asleep for two hours.

I'll just go back to sleep. I'll be back up in five minutes, and then I will get going, Emma tells herself, but she knows that it's no use. If she falls back asleep now, she'll be asleep much longer than five minutes.

She tucks her iced hands into her coat, rubbing them together to warm them up. Winter is coming, and that means colder mornings she will have to deal with. She doesn't need a mirror to know that her hair is rattled and frizzy, and her face is dark and tired. She stands up, looking up and down the dark alleyway she slept in. Despite her headache, she runs down the alley, chills running down her spine. It's especially cold this morning.

Emma's still a long way away from Silana, and she needs to make plans so she can get in and out of there undetected, preferably with Shawn and Sophia alive. Hopefully, they have no clue what's going on right now, but they soon will.

As she starts the day's journey on foot, Emma hopes that this time she won't fail her mission.

~

Sophia

KA-BAM!

The beaten up white volleyball sails over the towering net. Of all the places it could go, the ball comes zipping towards me like a bullet. "Drat! Somebody get it!" a girl on my team shouts. This person is thinking ahead; everybody knows I always miss if I try to get the ball. It's now coming closer and closer. Before I have the chance to hit it, though, the boy to my left jumps in front of me. He skids onto the wooden floor and extends his arms. It seems like he won't get it, but at the last second, he barely hits the ball and it flies straight back over the net. I breathe a sigh of relief. It's now the other team's problem.

Unfortunately, my relief is short-lived.

"Sophie Lorain!" a deep, angry voice calls from the sidelines. *Oh, great.* I think. *It's Coach Gime. Please don't be too mad at me!* I look over to where he is standing on the sideline. He is glaring down at me, with a frown painted across his face.

"It's Sophia," I whisper, not wanting anybody to hear me. Coach Gime has a knack for getting my name wrong.

Then the yelling begins. Now, I have to pay attention to what he's saying *and* the game that's going on. "Can you actually do something useful? Next time, when the ball comes your way, you'd better hit it or you get 100 pushups!" he shouts. *Yeah, yeah. Be more useful,* I think, but I know it's no use. He'll never get my name right and I'll never be good at volleyball.

I have to force myself not to yell at him and purposefully mispronounce his name. People always think it's Coach "Gimme," but students learn on their first day at this school that the "E" is silent.

I focus back on the game. The boy who saved the ball has already hopped back up, ready to save it again if need be. His wavy coffee-colored hair is all over his face and is sticking up in odd places. His bright blue eyes shine. This is Shawn, who is probably the best volleyball player in the entire school. He's been put into a class of younger kids so he can "Show them how it's done." He's as popular as he is good at volleyball. Most girls giggle and melt whenever he walks by them, because they consider him dreamy and hot. I don't, though. Actually, I can't think he is dreamy and hot. Shawn is my brother.

BAM! The ball comes flying back again. Luckily, this time, it's not near me. A girl named Jennifer hits it to a boy in the front row, and he sets it over the net. Then, someone on the other side spikes it back. What do you know? There's Shawn again, appearing out of nowhere. He slides across the floor and hits the ball back over the net with ease.

Maybe I won't end up doing pushups. Shawn's done me the favor of getting the ball for me whenever I need to. He knows I'll probably just mess something up and make everyone angry at me if I try.

"Sophia!" someone hisses. It's the girl to the right of me, Jennifer. She pushes me forward. "We're rotating!" Great, now I'm in the front row. I know that I have to keep even more concentrated now. Over to my right, Shawn is in the middle. Again, I hope he can cover for me.

The last thing I want to do now is play volleyball, but I'm stuck in this stupid Physical Training class for an hour and a half each day. There's nothing I can do about it. It's all because my school makes me do it.

See, my school is basically a giant mega-military boarding school, with about 5,000 students attending. Here, we have kids ranging from seven to eighteen. You start out in Year A, where the youngest kids are, and end up graduating in Year K. I'm in Year G and Shawn is in Year H. No matter what age you are, you're expected to be good with sports and weapons so we can go off into the military for our country, Lochbion.

ANIVERSI

Here, you're basically already in the army. You're trained from your first year here, Year A, to be up at 5:25 A.M. sharp. You have an hour and a half of Physical Training every day. When you're older, you learn how to handle weapons, so you can join the army as soon as you graduate. It seems like the dream school for somebody who wants to join the military when they get older. Unfortunately, that person is not me. This place is definitely not my dream school.

I am taken out of my daze and lose my train of thought when the ball makes its way towards me again. Quickly, I hold out my arms, ready to hit it, but it slams itself onto the wooden floor, three feet away from me. My team groans.

"Lorain! Last warning!" Coach Gime belts. "Pay attention!"

There is a KA-BUMP! of the ball being served by the other team. The ball comes flying back to our half of the court. Groaning, I look forward. I really try to pay attention now. Jennifer sets the ball back to the other side. The people on the other side start trying to get the ball over here.

It all happens too fast. My body can't control itself as it comes crashing to the ground. The ball has hit me square in the temple. My head is pounding as a wave of dizziness cascades upon me. As everything fades to darkness, I can only hear one thing: laughter.

~

When I become conscious again, I immediately open my eyes and examine my surroundings. I'm in the school's healing center. This is where they take injured and sick students, and obviously, try to heal them.

I'm on a small bed, and there's a freezing ice pack wrapped in a towel on my head. Over to my right, there is someone talking to the nurse. It's Coach Gime.

I quickly shut my eyes. I don't want to talk to him. He might give me pushups, despite the fact I'm not in class.

I listen to what he says, and it surprises me.

"Is she okay?" he asks. Is this real? Did Coach Gime actually show concern for me? How can he care about me when I'm the laughing stock of my Year?

"It looks like she'll be fine. What happened to her?" the nurse asks.

"She got hit in the temple by a spike," Coach Gime explains.

"Ouch. That hurts," says the nurse.

"I have to go," Coach Gime says. "I've got another class. It's Year A students. You know how that works. Those little ankle biters."

I can hear Coach opening the door. The creak sends shivers down my spine and a ringing sound in my head. He shuts the door, and I hear the nurse go back to what she was doing.

ANIVERSI

Now that he's gone, I open my eyes again. I try to sit up, but there's an ache that sweeps through my head that prevents me from doing so. Then, the nurse notices I'm awake. She stands up and comes over to me.

"Well, sweetie, you've been out for a while," she says.

"How long?" I ask.

"Let's see. . ." she checks the black clock sitting on her desk. "Only a couple of hours. It's good you're finally awake. We've checked, and you don't have a concussion, but don't be surprised if you get a few headaches over the next few days."

"Look at how lame I am," I say. "I got knocked out by a volleyball."

The nurse ignores my comment. "You can go back to class whenever you feel better," she says. "Classes will end in about an hour and a half."

"Fine," I mumble. I lie back down.

I'm starting to feel much better, but honestly, I don't want to go back to class. I turn over and look out the glass door of the healing center into the hallway. What will my classmates say about me now? They'll never let me forget this. It is things like being knocked out by a volleyball that makes my classmates shun me and hate me.

All schools have a hierarchy with kids that are popular and kids that aren't, and I happen to be at the bottom of this one. It's just, the problem is, how is Shawn on the top? I'm his sister, so shouldn't I be up there with him? Come to think of it, he really is popular. I feel a pang of jealousy. What would it be like to be with the cool kids?

I have to remind myself that I don't care what the popular kids are all about: sports. At least I shouldn't care. *You'd have to be athletic to be with them,* I remember. Does Shawn realize he's popular simply because he can save a volleyball?

As I wonder about my school's hierarchy, a few more minutes pass. I make myself stop thinking about being popular and sit up. My head doesn't feel the sharp pain it did last time, so I go ahead and stand. I feel a bit wobbly at first, but I then walk over to where the nurse is sitting at her desk.

"You still have one class left. It starts in fifteen minutes," she says, not looking up from her computer. "You should get going."

"Sure," I say. I don't want to make up any more classwork than I already have to. I walk over to the glass door. I can see my reflection in it. There's my Physical Training uniform; a gray school shirt with mesh green shorts, and then there's my dark curly hair and bright blue eyes, the same that Shawn has.

I open the door and decide to go back to class. I walk down the hallways, with full classrooms of small children raising their hands or writing on worksheets. These are the years A through D. Next, as I get deeper into the school, I hit a forest of lockers which signifies the middle years; E through G. I wander the familiar path to my locker and punch in the code with the glass keypad without even thinking about it. I grab my school uniform I need to change into before I get to class.

When I look at a clock, I still have ten minutes before the bell rings and everybody floods into the hallway, going to their next class. I want to get to my next period on time, so I hurry up and take my bag with me into the nearest restroom to change.

Promptly after changing, the bell rings, so I go back to my locker and get my little tablet; the device that holds all my textbooks and papers, and I head off to my last class of the day: History of Lochbion.

I want to enter class and be unseen. It's probably likely. Most people have been ignoring me since my first day here, when they figured out that I wasn't very good at sports. Normally, I'm cool with this situation since I'm not a very sociable person in the first place, but the unexpected happens and immediately, snide remarks make their way to me.

"Look. It's Sophia. We missed you," somebody says sarcastically. I trudge over to my seat. More people begin filing in, and with this, more people say rude things.

"Wow, look! It's the girl who's afraid of a volleyball! Can I have an autograph?"

I attempt keep calm, which is difficult to do when everybody is ganging up on me.

"Look. Even the volleyball hates her. It just smacked her in the face and BAM! Out cold," someone cuts in again. They may as well go get a knife from the weaponry room and slice it down my spine.

"She's a Transmorgifer. No wonder," somebody spits. I give this person a quizzical look. *What's a Transmorgifer?* I think.

"What kind of a name is that?" I ask. This person looks at me like I'm crazy that I don't know what transmogi-whatever is. Should I know? Did I miss out on something?

"You better shut up," somebody else says, staring daggers at me. "You're lucky we haven't killed you yet. Too bad we have to wait."

I want to say something, but I'm speechless.

It takes a few moments for me to process what they're saying. Kill me? Are they crazy? Am I crazy? I can't even compute the thought. I didn't know my classmates hated me *this* much. Even so, I was just knocked out by a volleyball. I could be hallucinating. That's most likely it. I take these strange and sudden death threats and brush them off my shoulders. Either they were kidding or I'm hallucinating really badly.

The bell rings. The forty students in the room file into desks as the teacher enters the room.

"Quiet down," he says. The random chattering stops. "I hope you all turned in your unit predictions assignment. You're not going to understand anything I talk about today unless you did." I look around the room. A handful people twitch in surprise, as if they were saying aloud, *It was due today?* It's obvious they've forgotten.

"Today, we will begin a new unit. We've talked about the countries that used to inhabit this continent we live in right now, which has led to the discovery of Uranium, and the beginning of nuclear bombs. Now, we'll move onto exactly how North America ended up as our country," he begins lecturing.

I can see about ten people rolling their eyes. We already know what happened. "Hard workers for a better future" *have* to know about these sorts of things. Why must he tell us again? The few students who silently complain don't stop him from telling us.

And so he begins. A bit more than 200 years ago, people found out about the atomic bomb. There was a giant war going on, and two of them were used to stop the fighting.

Afterwards, a giant length of time passed, but the United States, which used to be part of the continent we're on, set off two of them again. After this, a ripple effect eventually happened. One thing lead to another, and it started World War III.

There was mass destruction, death, and huge amounts of radiation. Both North and South America had been bombed with enough bombs to kill almost everybody. The land had become so radiated, everybody had to move to the small area where the radiation hadn't affected: the land surrounding the Great Lakes. The few people still living in North America banded together and decided to start from scratch. During this meeting the remaining people had, they realized that they had messed up too much before, so there was a unanimous vote to start an entirely new country. They called it Lochbion, which has roots that mean "Place of Life."

Then the teacher begins lecturing about the principles our country was founded in: to create hard workers for a better future. Yep, that's basically the slogan. "Hard workers for a better future."

"In the United States, people were viewed as lazy and arrogant," he explains to us. "So the people decided to take away that old stereotype and replace it with a new one."

Yes, we already know this! Now I want to complain too. By the looks on everybody's faces, about half the class wants to join me. Does he realize this knowledge has been engraved into our brains since we've been able to talk? Does he realize that in order to create "hard workers for a better future," we have to know the history of our country?

He then begins lecturing us about the formation of the six different Sectors, which are basically the states of this country. I live in Sector Four.

However, the teacher doesn't fool us. I figured out when I was seven the only reason the Sectors serve is to keep kids in school. No, it's not to keep people in different Sectors from fraternizing with each other or as a punishment or whatever, but simply to keep the children in school. (Lame, I know.) See, you need an ID to get move from Sector to Sector. You need to be eighteen and have a school diploma before you can get one, though. The Sectors are so small, your only choice is to stay in school. The government's very strict and serious about this hard worker people idea.

The teacher starts to tell us about Mt. Dalorn, which isn't really a mountain. It's just the nickname for Sector Six. How it got its nickname, nobody knows. Anyway, Mt. Dalorn is where all the serious government business happens. From what I hear, there is zero goofing off there. The adults deal with complicated government matters, and the kids who live there go to schools that specialize in helping them eventually deal with complicated government matters. Before the teacher can get into detail, the sound of the bell cuts him off. I grab my tablet, stand up, and begin filing out. I don't want to talk to anybody. The comment about wanting to kill me has scared me a little bit.

Unfortunately, I'm not so lucky. "Be warned, Sophia," a girl whispers to me as we leave the room. It's Jennifer, the girl who was on my volleyball team earlier. "I can't wait to get rid of you." She has a sinister smile on her face, and something tells me she's not joking.

My mouth begins speaking before I can stop it. "Okay, not funny. Don't really kill me," I say.

Jennifer stands there for a moment, but then a wave of confusion runs through her face. "Fine, I won't-" but she doesn't finish her sentence. She leaves the room, with a baffled look plastered on her face.

She's not the only one who's baffled. Are my classmates really out to kill me?

Chapter 2

~

Emma

Downtown Silana is crazy in the late afternoon. There's cars inching by, people pushing past, and towering buildings everywhere. Emma heard that Sophia and Shawn's campus is somewhere in the middle of town, but she's not sure. As she strolls along the sidewalk, she tries to figure out a way to find their school without being detected.

She's now becoming very nervous. She doesn't even know where their school is, and yet she's heard word that the government already Brainwashed the school. They know what Sophia and Shawn are.

What is she going to do when she gets there? Talk the principal out of attacking Sophia and Shawn? Talk the school out of it? She's no good at Brainwashing others, so how is she going to cancel out something more powerful?

As she keeps going, the possibility of her mission failing seems to becoming higher and higher.

~

Sophia

As I slowly make my way out of the classroom, I decide that hallucination is the only solution to my problem. *I might have a concussion after all,* I think. *Or maybe not. I wouldn't be able to pay attention in class if I had a concussion.* As I wonder about brain injuries, one thing is for sure: the volleyball must've hit me pretty hard, because the thought of my classmates wanting to kill me is completely and utterly absurd. They don't necessarily appreciate my presence, but killing me is a little bit overboard.

I begin making my way back to my dorm, going through hallways of people stopping at lockers to drop off tablets or getting clothes for sports practice. I don't need to stop at my locker. I have my tablet with me, and I plan to do my extra work.

I'd love to go through the hallway un-noticed. Lucky for me, nobody typically talks to me, so I can have time to ponder these strange threats I've received in silence.

I soon realize I'm not heading to the girl's dorm rooms, but instead in the direction of Shawn's locker. He must have at least a few moments before he has practice. Perhaps he can help me get a grasp on reality.

"Shawn!" I call as I see him. I push my way through the crowd, heading towards him. He turns around from his locker and smiles when he sees me. My heart jumps inside. It's nice to have somebody care about me and not threaten to kill me.

"Hey," he says, putting his tablet in his bag. "I'm sorry you got knocked out at Physical Training today. You okay?"

"Yeah," I say, knowing full well I'm telling a big, fat lie, but I'll explain my problem to him later.

"Apparently I'm now known as the girl who's afraid of the volleyball," I say. We begin walking towards the gym, where he has basketball practice.

"Well, are you afraid of a volleyball?" asks Shawn.

"Of course not," I reply.

"They why do you let it bother you?" he smiles. That makes me think for a moment. *Why do you let it bother you, then?* I don't want to answer his question, because honestly, I don't know the answer myself. The hallways are clearing up, and we're now in front of the boy's changing room.

"I guess you have to go," I say, purposefully avoiding his query.

"I'll see you tonight," Shawn says as he hugs me. "I have to get to practice."

"Okay," I say. He heads into the locker room.

I head off to my dorm feeling happier than usual. As I walk out of the building where classes are held, I can feel the icy wind dancing around my face. The buttery sunlight shines down, and I have to squin to see properly. The trees on campus have leaves that are changing color. Autumn is here, but I can already feel the winter weather coming.

I approach the two dorm buildings; there's one for girls and one for boys. Both of the buildings are very large and tall. There's a floor for each Year, so they're both 11 stories high. Their metal exterior gives off a cool glow from the sun.

I head inside the building where the girls stay, and make my way to the glass elevator. There's another girl who comes in the elevator with me, and the door shuts.

At first, she doesn't recognize me, but I recognize her almost immediately. Although I can't put a name on the face, I know this girl is one of the boy-crazy girls in Year G with me. She has a particular obsession with obtaining my brother as a boyfriend. This is a girl who cares solely about being popular and flirting with Shawn, and nothing else. "Hard workers for a better future" doesn't always apply to everyone.

Then, the girl recognizes me. She doesn't say a thing and looks petrified for a moment. She bites her lip and it becomes really awkward. Oh, it must be terrible, right? Having to be in an elevator with the girl who's afraid of the volleyball. The awkwardness breaks as the doors open. I know we're on Floor 7, the floor where my Year stays. The Shawn-obsessed girl bolts away from me as fast as she can.   Since there are so many of us, there are four different hallways. My room is in the first one, so it's a quick run down the hall to the dorm where I live. Just like the lockers, there is a glass keypad built into the door. I punch in the five digit code, and it opens.

ANIVERSI

After I enter, I slide up into my bunk and turn on my tablet. I attempt to start my homework, but the door opens again. It's Liz, one of my three roommates. A normal person would greet the other upon entering a room, but I know I'll get no response.

She's just here to get some clothes she can go to sports practice in. She grabs them and quickly leaves, as if I was never here. Fine with me. It's better than being threatened about death.

Now, I begin my extra work I have to get done.

~

While most people are off with sports practice, I actually have time to get the large amount of work the teachers assign us completed right after classes end. After I finish, it is just about time for dinner, so I start heading to the dining room, which is right next to the main building.

There's nobody in the elevator. Good. No one to give me death threats.

Tonight for dinner, there is a plate of rice with a rich beef stew on top, all drizzled in gravy. Sweaty, hungry kids begin filing into line, most of them having come from various sports practices.

After getting my food, I get a glass of water, and head over to a small table near the window. This is where I normally sit. Shawn is already waiting there. The fact that he is sitting here is partly why I think he deserves the Brother of the Year Award. He gives up sitting with his friends to sit with his little sister, and yet he still manages to stay on top of the popularity ladder.

"How's it going?" I ask.

"Going great," he says. "Practice was awesome. I shot four three-pointers."

"Awesome," I say. I take a bite of stew. Even though I'm not 100 percent sure what a three-pointer is, it's nice to have somebody to talk to.

"And how are you?" he asks. I almost choke on my bite of food. I desperately want to tell him what's been going on, but I'm not sure this is the right time to do that. Somebody could over hear us, so I decide to change the subject.

"Wow. I love this meal." I say.

"Yah, Mhee twho," Shawn agrees, a bite of stew in his mouth. He swallows.

"You didn't answer my question," he says.

"What question?"

"How are you?"

"I . . . I'll tell you later," I say. "We can talk after dinner."

"Excuse me?" a voice grumbles behind me. I get a tap on the shoulder. "Sophia Lorain?"

"That's me," I say. I turn around and see the person I least want to see. The vice principal of the school. He is extremely tall, and his colorless hair and colorless eyes make him look even more intimidating. This is Mr. Smith: the scariest vice principal in the world.

"You're not in uniform," he grunts at Shawn.

"I had sports practice," Shawn says, but Mr. Smith just glares at him.

"Sophia, you're needed in the office," he says. He grabs my wrist and takes me away before I can even object.

"Meet me!" Shawn calls.

"Okay," I yell back, but by now I'm twenty yards from him and out of the dining hall.

Mr. Smith drags me across the lawn over to the main building where the offices are, and where the principal is. *Am I in trouble? I wonder what I did wrong,* I think. A wave of panic runs through me when I remember the death threats I received earlier today. Does this Transfornigra-thingy have anything to do with it?

Mr. Smith drops me off in front of the Principal's office and leaves promptly. I gulp. With a trembling hand, I grab the handle to the door. I'm about to enter, but I hear voices inside. There seems to be a girl, about thirteen or fourteen, talking to the principal. I don't recognize her voice.

"You're not going to turn her in. They'll kill her," says the girl. I let go of the handle and my palms start sweating. This is sounding a lot like the death threats I received earlier.

"Fine! I won't-" the principal sounds confused for a moment. "Wait a minute. No. I have to," he says.

"That doesn't matter!" the girl barks back. "You're not going to turn her in!"

"The vice principal is getting her right now! Too late!" he says, with another hint of confusion in his voice. What makes him so confused? Is it something this girl is saying?

"There have been rumors of another one," the principal says.

"You will not turn her in," the girl says firmly. "You're going to make me do something I don't want to do," she says.

Suddenly, strange sounds start coming from the room. BANG!

"Guuuhhh," says the Principal. I can hear the girl climbing out the window. *What happened in there*? I open the door a bit.

What I see inside makes me want to scream. The principal is knocked out, just as I was earlier today, but there is a small stream of blood trickling from his forehead. I close the door immediately. The deciding factor has been made. I am hallucinating. The principal cannot be knocked out, and I cannot be sane. I open the door again just to make sure.

He is still there, out cold. A firm hand grasps my shoulder and I turn around to see Vice Principal Smith. Now I'm really in trouble. I've been caught red-handed when I didn't even do the crime.

ANIVERSI

"What is going on in there?" he bellows. He opens the door, and cries out, seeing the principal slumped on his desk.

"What did you do?" he yells.

"I didn't do anything!" I yell back. After this comment, Mr. Smith completely ignores me, and proceeds to phone the nurse from the healing center.

It's as if I'm not even here. I was just caught moments after the principal was knocked out, and now I'm ignored? Everything going through my head is all jumbled up, and I'm sick of death threats and dying. It's starting to give me a throbbing headache.

"Sophia!" says the nurse as she enters. "What are you doing here?" You need to be back in your dorm! It's after dinner."

"Yes, Lorain," says Mr. Smith. "Head on back."

All right. I'm fine with not getting in trouble, but I was hardly accused in the first place. My head begins to throb more, and I run back to my dorm as fast as I can.

~

I close the door to my room. It's 8 p.m. now, which means that we're all supposed to be on our floors. Liz, Ellie, and Isabel, my roommates, are here already. I take a deep breath and I cross the tiny room we share. I climb up into my bunk, trying to take in what just happened. I'm a complete wreck, and I don't care if my roommates see.

The principal got knocked out by a weird stranger. I almost get framed, and by simply saying "I didn't do anything," I was claimed innocent. I've been knocked out by a spike and I've had about five death threats today. What is going on with me?

"Ooh, look at her," says Ellie. Liz and Isabel chuckle. *Wow,* I think. *It's a miracle. They're acknowledging my presence!* The fact that they're pushing at my buttons doesn't help at all.

"Come on Ellie, she's supposed to be the Transmorgifer!" says Liz.

"Aww, why can't we kill her right now?" whines Isabel.

I somehow manage not to scream at them. After all that's been happening today, I don't need any more death threats. I don't need any more strange events. I yank off my necktie that the school makes us wear and hang it around my bedpost. I quickly grab my pajamas from the closet and exit the dorm room. I storm down the hallway to the huge shower room on Floor 7. If there are people there, I don't notice them. It's high time I ignore somebody instead of somebody ignoring me.

The room is warm and steamy from students washing up before bed. There are ten rows of ten showers each. I zoom into a random stall and I take a long, hot shower. I try to let the worries of the day go down with the water into the drain. I keep trying to convince myself I hit my head way too hard on that volleyball; I *must* be hallucinating.

I wait until there are no more voices in the room before shutting the water off. After drying my hair with a towel and dressing into my pajamas, I've finally convinced myself that I'm going crazy. I'm just going to have to deal with it somehow.

I step into my slippers and walk back towards my room. When I enter, I see Liz, Ellie and Isabel are asleep. Ellie is even snoring.

Then the final thing that just about pushes me over the edge appears.

There is a large, gray dog standing in the middle of my room. A dog. In the middle of my room. Pets are strictly forbidden on campus, so how in the world is there one here? I blink my eyes and look agin. Yes, it is a *dog.* At first it doesn't see me, but then it jerks its head over to where I am. It has been standing next to my bed, sniffing my tie.

"Go away, you stupid dog. I've had enough hallucinations today," I moan. The dog *winks* at me, and then it goes over to the open window of my dorm. It then climbs up onto the window sill, and then jumps straight out of the window. Seven stories down. I run across the room and I can see it scamper away in the moonlight. There is no way it could have survived that.

"Okay, Sophia," I tell myself. "You're officially crazy." Wide eyed, I climb back up onto my top bunk, knowing that I won't get any sleep tonight.

Chapter 3

~

Emma

Emma hates having to leave Sophia and Shawn. If she was caught on campus, they'd arrest her immediately because she's near the top of the most wanted list in Lochbion. (Don't ask . . . It's a long story.)

When she entered the school grounds, she attempted to reason with the principal. She's not that good at Brainwashing herself, but she tried. From what she could tell, they were just about to begin the attack right then, but that's seeming less and less likely now. Hopefully her feeble attempts at Brainwashing will delay the attack a day or two, if she's lucky.

She's nervous they might attack right now anyway.

Emma has a way of identifying Sophia, now, so she has to clear out. She'll eventually find Sophia and Shawn.

If they don't die first.

~

Sophia

My failed attempts at sleeping during the night make me extremely drowsy in the morning. At 5:25 A.M., the loud, obnoxious alarm goes off throughout the whole building through the speakers. This is everybody's cue to get up and scramble out into the hallway before inspection comes. I jump awake at the piercing noise, but my body immediately begs to lie back down. I know better, though. Sleeping in gives you automatic detention for a week. As I slump out of bed and trudge out of the dorm into the hallway, I can hear Ellie, Isabel, and Liz whispering. Goodness only knows what they're talking about.

Then comes Mrs. Moraine; she's the inspector of hallway 1. Whatever small talk and chatter there was in the first place immediately dies down into a sustained silence. If a pin would fall right now, everybody would hear it. All of the girls in hallway 1 know how ruthless Mrs. Moraine is.

Then, the yelling begins. I think she might be saying something about standing up straight, but I'm too tired to be paying any attention. I gaze forward, daydreaming about how nice it would be to have twenty more minutes in bed. Moments later, Liz shakes my shoulder. She points towards Mrs. Moraine.

"Lorain!" she calls. "What are you doing? Do you think that slouching is acceptable?" I jolt out of my fantasy and rub my eyes. I stop slouching and look forward. A few more moments pass. These are the crucial moments where you must stay completely silent and still before she releases us.

"You are dismissed. Breakfast is at 6:30. You'd better not be tardy!" she yells. We shuffle back into our rooms to get ready for the day.

After entering my dorm, I open the closet I share with my roommates. I take out the uniform all of the girls are to wear. There's a bleach white blouse, an olive green plaid skirt with a matching tie, and a jet-black cardigan. As I get my tie hanging off my bunk, I freeze for a moment. The strange memories of yesterday are flooding back into my brain. The threats. The principal. The dog.

My head starts swelling in pain as I think of everything that's happened, so I try to distract myself by doing something else. I comb out my frizzy, curly hair, and brush my teeth in the tiny powder room adjacent to our dorm.

It's now 5:57. Outside my window, the sky is turning gray; the sun is just about to start rising. I can hear Liz and Ellie giggling about something again. Isabel is laughing and making a joke about the neckties students must wear.

"Don't you just hate it," she says, "When you enter a room with these stupid ties, and you're trying to be handsome because these ties are like, soooo manly, and then some smoking hot boy comes in and handsomes better than you can?"

"Did you just turn the word handsome into a verb?" Liz asks. I'm surprised Liz actually knows what a verb is. She's laughing so hard her face is turning red. The girls giggle some more. As I listen, it shocks me that only a few hours ago, these people were threatening to kill me. Now they're joking around about ties. *No,* I think. I shove the thought out of my brain. My head is starting to hurt again.

Ignoring the rest of their conversation, I decide to go downstairs early. My roommates certainly won't miss me. Hopefully, I can meet up with Shawn and make up the time we were going to spend together the previous night. I have to tell him what's been going on with these wonderful death threats I've been receiving. I exit the room and head down the hallway to the elevator. Only a couple of students are making their way over to breakfast this early.

After going down the elevator and exiting the girl's dorm building, I start looking for Shawn. It would be great if he decides to come down early this morning.

I see plenty other classmates of mine, but I don't see Shawn. These other people are either sitting or standing on the campus lawn, and they're just chatting with each other. It seems like such a normal thing to do, but I am amazed by it. It may seem creepy, but since almost no one bothers to talk to me, I sometimes watch and see how they talk to each other.

I plop myself down in the cold, dewy grass and watch a group of four or five students talk. I can see them more clearly as the sun starts to rise.

Talking with friends seems natural, but not to me. I figure I would have at least some friends, but in reality, I don't know how to talk with people. (Shawn is the only exception. Period.) Obviously, I know how to speak, but I don't know what to say or how to say it or when to say it. Another reason why I watch everybody talk to each other: if I have to speak with somebody, I don't completely mess up what I'm trying to say.

The sun is creeping up the horizon now, and heavy clouds in the distance suggest that today might be a stormy one. Shawn hasn't turned up yet. I figured he would get my telepathic sibling message I sent to him: *Meet me downstairs early! We have to talk!*

The sun begins slowly creeping along the sky. Shawn doesn't come down, so I decide head to the dining hall. I'll definitely see him there. Breakfast this morning is scrambled eggs, toast, and fruit. I don't see Shawn as I sit down at our usual table with my plate, and I'm beginning to get a little bit worried about him, but he comes only a few moments later. He sits down next to me with his plate.

He immediately begins to apologize. "Sorry I'm so late, Sop-" but he is cut off by the loudspeaker.

"Attention students!" a voice calls, but this isn't any voice. This is the *principal*. He was knocked out just yesterday evening! I'm glad I haven't eaten anything yet, because I'm beginning to feel sick. I thought the principal was going to "turn me in."

No. No. No, I think. *You will not think of that. You're just crazy in the head.*

"Classes will be starting in forty-five minutes. Some of you have begun to think it's funny to be tardy to class. I certainly don't, and I don't appreciate it at all. Teachers now have permission to give out detentions for any student who is late to class," he says. There is a collective groan throughout the room as he hangs up from the loudspeaker. The rest of breakfast goes by quickly and quietly, because nobody wants to be tardy for class. I don't eat anything, because I've completely lost all my appetite.

"We should probably get going," I tell Shawn as he finishes up his plate. "Don't want to be tardy." I'm never tardy anyways.

He nods slowly in agreement. "I'll see you after classes end. Will you meet me at my locker?"

"Sure," I say. "Today's your day off from sports practice, right? We have to talk as soon as school ends." He nods, and we part our ways to get to our classes.

Looking at the time, it's 7:10. I have five minutes to get to my first period. Ever so conveniently, the room is on the other side of the middle year hallways, so I have to speed-walk so I can make it there in time.

I step through the doors of the science lab just as the tardy bell rings.

I stride over to my lab seat. On the board is the funny quote of the day, being projected wirelessly from Mrs. Grint's tablet. The quote of the day can have anything to do with science, as long as it's funny. It says, "What do you do with a dead chemist? Barium!" Snickers and laughs echo throughout the room as the students read the quote and discuss it. I can't help but smile myself.

Mrs. Grint starts taking attendance. For all those who don't know, (If you don't, I'd like to know where you've been all this time.) both Mrs. Grint and her husband teach here. Mrs. Grint does science, and Mr. Grint, math. Anybody who's anyone knows that to be cool, you have to have at least one of them as your teacher. It's probably because Mr. and Mrs. Grint are just plain cool themselves. They've only been teaching here for three years, and it's already unspoken law that anyone that doesn't have a class with them should be jealous of those who do. Shawn is lucky. He has both Mr. and Mrs. Grint, which only adds to his coolness factor.

After scrolling through the first few students on her list, Mrs. Grint eventually reaches me. "Sophia Lorain," she calls, smiling.

"Present," I call back. Mrs. Grint gets my name right every time, unlike a certain Physical Training coach I could mention.

"I hope you guys didn't eat a rich breakfast this morning," Mrs. Grint says after she finishes.

"Why?" a few students call out.

Mrs. Grint laughs. "Because today we will be dissecting frogs." A few students groan. I'm not one of them, but that doesn't mean I don't want to dissect this frog.

"Now, don't start complaining," Mrs. Grint says. "We've already done the fish. Was that as awful as you thought it was?"

The groaning stops. Dissecting the fish two days ago wasn't as nearly as awful as I thought it would be. It was actually pretty cool once I got used to it. Maybe this frog won't be so bad after all.

"Pull up the Year G science page on the network on your tablets. There's a list of places you must identify, a guide on where to make the incisions, and a place to turn in your drawing you will make on your tablet after you're done," she explains to us.

"Go get aprons and safety goggles. Then, report to me to collect your dissection kits. Remember, you're in Year G, and you have to be mature about this. Show those Year F kids how it's done!" She smiles. She presses a small circular button on her desk. The closet in the back of the room opens up, and there are racks of aprons and piles of high-tech anti-fog and anti-splatter safety glasses. There's a race to the back closet to get the aprons and glasses.

After obtaining an apron, safety goggles, and a dissection kit, Mrs. Grint pairs me up with a boy named Spenser. I've never talked to him, and when I say, "Hi,"

"Sorry, Spenser," another boy says to him. "Hope you'll survive with *her*," he spits. He doesn't have the decency to even say my name.

Spenser and I walk over to one of the twenty lab stations, and sitting there in the blue dissection tray is a dead frog. I set my tablet down next to it. Quickly, I pull up the instructions on incisions we need to make. "Look," I say. "We need to make a bilateral incision-"

But Spenser's already making the incision, completely ignoring me. *Okay, cool with me,* I think as he spends a while trying to actually make the cut. Meanwhile, I simply stand there, doing nothing.

"Remember, don't let one person do all the work!" Mrs. Grint calls to the class, eying Spenser. He's finally done now. He groans, gives me the surgical scissors, and I make the two other slits. I can hear Mrs. Grint turn on some music to pump up the process.

After we make the incisions, we start pinning the frog down so we can see the insides. "Looking at the guide, I think that small organ right there's the heart, and those are the lungs," I say, pointing at the frog.

Spenser nods. He's already taken the drawing module on our tablets and is drawing the outline of the frog. He labels the organs.

I sigh, and I take out the drawing module on my tablet. Trembling, I start to draw the frog. The insides are pretty disgusting. Looking around, I can see that no other student seems to think the same. Maybe it's just that Mrs. Grint has sugarcoated the grossness of it, or maybe it's just that Mrs. Grint is the one teaching the class.

"I believe the gall bladder's under here," I say, pointing to the lungs.

"Yeah," he whispers. He prods at the frog with a pointer, examining something.

"How's it going?" A friendly voice asks. Mrs. Grint has turned up at my station.

"Great," says Spenser. He's absorbed in his drawing on his tablet and refuses to even look up.

After I finish my drawing, I clean up the lab station and answer the reflection questions Mrs. Grint posted for us. Once I'm doing with the questions, I switch my tablet off and wait for the class to end.

Mrs. Grint approaches me. She's probably going to ask me if I'm finished, but she stops right next to me. She leans over close to my ear. "We're going to turn you in," she whispers. I freeze. I don't know what to say.

Isn't that what the principal said yesterday?

They're going to turn me in?

What did I do?

Things start to get really weird when Spenser says, "She's right. Transmorgifer." He spits.

"Yeah, I heard that you've been breaking the law," says the girl across from me.

"What?" I ask.

"You're the Transmorgifer everyone's been talking about," says Spenser, glaring at me. I have only a little bit of self-control left, but it's enough to stop me from screaming. I want to go back to when everybody ignored me. I'd like that better than all this attention and death threats.

"Then, why aren't we turning her in?" asks the girl across from me. I think her name's Gwen.

"Just a minute," says Spenser. "I just need to finish this drawing. Then we break out the weapons." After this comment, I really feel like screaming, so that is what I do.

You're crazy, I think as I run to the door and wrench it open, frantically trying to leave the room before I get any more death threats.

I sprint down the hall, desperate to get out of the school, or at least to the nurse's office where I can take some crazy-person medication. Maybe I can just knock myself out again and hope none of this ever happened.

I'm almost at the end of the hallway when I hear cries behind me. My classmates are chasing me. They must be serious about wanting to kill me.

But they're not the only ones screaming.

"We're going to kill you!" I hear yells from another class, and then I see Shawn sprinting towards me from another hallway.

"SHAWN!" I shriek.

"SOPHIA!" he shouts.

That's when we hear the screaming. Hollers come from our two classes. They're right on our tails. The sound grows louder as increased amount of classes join in the rampage. The whole school must be chasing us.

At a moment like this, the only thing I really want to do is sit down, curl up in a ball, and cry. It sounds stupid, but I'm so freaked out and stressed out, I'm just about to, but when I turn around, I see my classmates have surgical scissors and scalpels. This, and the huge amount of adrenaline and energy coursing through my body, is the only thing keeping me going.

Although running isn't on the list of strengths I have, running in these stupid dress shoes they have us wear is even worse. I take a moment to slow down and yank them off, so I'm running simply in socks.

As we are chased down the winding hallways, we end up in the younger Years. As we zip past those, we can hear the cry of younger kids- 6, 7, and 8 year olds join the pursuit for us. This makes me sad. Do they even know why they're chasing us?

Somehow, I, being the most physically un-sporty person in the entire Sector Four, manage to keep up with Shawn. He's probably the fastest runner in the school. I tell myself it's the adrenaline that's running through my body, but deep down I know it's something more complex than that.

Soon, we've exited the building and ran onto campus. I have drowned out the sound of the people chasing us, and I'm concentrating solely on getting as far away as I can from this place. My heart is pumping, my palms sweating, and my feet still seem to be running. What's wrong with me? How is it that I can do this?

I sprint across the grass, still covered in dew, and the socks I'm wearing get wet. Before I know it, I've reached the gates of the campus. I turn around for just a moment as Shawn climbs the gates. How can we be thirty yards ahead of the crowd? Shawn grabs my hand and helps me over.

"Sophia!" he yells, "Quick!" We're on top of the fence now, and we hastily jump off. He lands on his feet, but I collapse for half a second until I get back up again and I brush myself off. By now, the people chasing us have reached the gate. Spenser is at the front, clutching the scalpel. He chucks it at me, and I feel a searing pain in my lower right leg as it slashes across my body.

"GAH!" I screech. It has just scraped my leg, but it sears in hot pain anyway. Now is not the time to care about that sort of stuff. I catch up to Shawn, who is ten feet ahead of me.

"Shawn!" I yell. I grab his hand and we run.

I'm running through the streets of downtown Silana. It's one of the largest cities in Sector Four. That's good. We can lose the crowd behind us more easily. But there's also a good chance that Shawn and I could become separated.

There are cars slowly inching by on the road next to us. All around Shawn and I are tall, icy, sleek buildings. There are crowds and crowds of people making their way around town on foot, and we have to rush past them. We can't stop. These people who used to seem normal this morning, doing normal things like talking to each other. They aren't normal. They want to kill me.

I keep my hand locked into Shawn's.

We shove our way through more groups of people.

I keep going until I look behind myself and I don't see anybody from school threatening me with knives and scalpels. I stop Shawn for a moment. We take a look around for a moment as the crowds and people begin to shove past us. It seems as if we've

"Did we lose them?" I ask Shawn.

"I think so," he says.

I have no clue where we are, or how long we've been going. I sit down on a bench next to a building, and Shawn sits next to me.

"We need to talk," I tell him over the sound of the crowd and the city. "These people," I choke out, tears coming down my face, "have been threatening to kill me since yesterday. I think I'm going crazy." Shawn leans over to hug me and I shove my face into his shirt, trying to block out the rest of the world.

"Um, Sophia," Shawn says. "There's something you need to know."

"What?"

ANIVERSI

"They've been giving me death threats too."

~~

Chapter 4

~

Emma

Emma has completely cleared out of Silana. She's making her way to the town where Sophia and Shawn live: Weston. She figured that they would eventually turn up there. In all situations like this, the victims always flee to their own homes first.

But they could already be dead. Then she would've failed her mission, and that would make her growing list a total of three and a half failed missions. Emma goes through the drizzling weather, trying to figure out what to do and to calm herself.

She doesn't know the time, but Emma knows that the attack could happen any moment. Hopefully, her list of failed missions can stay at two and a half.

~

Sophia

"Really?" I ask Shawn, completely in disbelief.

"Yes," Shawn admits with a sad expression on his face. "I wanted to tell you, but I didn't know what to say."

"That's all right," I say. I stare down at my shoes and I notice the wound Spenser gave me. The blood is beginning to dry up. It still burns with pain although it's a small cut. "What do we do now?" I ask Shawn, staring at the minuscule trickle of blood slowly sliding down my leg.

"We should get a cab and go home," he says. "Mom and Dad can help us figure out what to do next."

"How are we going to pay the Mutary?" I ask him.

"I think I have a bit of change in my pocket we can use to pay. How about you?"

I check the small pocket in my skirt, and luckily enough, there's four one-merit bills in there. Shawn and I pool our money, and it comes out to twenty merits exactly. "Is that enough to get us home?" I ask him.

"We can get a start home," he says, and gets up from the bench we're sitting on.

Luckily, there are plenty of Mutaries with cabs who are willing to drive us. The Mutaries are the sad, depressing individuals who have failed at achieving the "hard worker for a better future" idea. Whether they were born extremely poor or didn't do well in school, Mutaries aren't respected within society. They're given the jobs left-over that nobody else wants like janitors or cab drivers. Most of them are just nice people in a bad situation. I figure they should get at least some credit for doing something, but most people treat the Mutaries like vermin.

Shawn stands up and pushes through the crowd. A cab appears almost out of nowhere, and Shawn flags it down.

Twenty merits can only take you so far. The cost for this taxi is one merit per mile, so we end up going twenty miles before Shawn and I have run out of merits. After staring out the window for half an hour and ignoring the feeling of blood drying on my leg, the Mutary stops the taxi.

"Sorry," he says, "I'm going to have to let you off here."

He kicks us out into the sidewalk, and drives off without further ado, leaving us penniless and nowhere to go. It's begun to drizzle, and the weather is cold and sad.

Shawn looks at me and I look at him. "Where do we go?" I ask him.

"Let's start there," Shawn says. He points to a convenience store a little bit down the road. "I don't think we'll be going back to school."

"Yeah, I don't think so either," I say. After taking one step, the scab beginning to form on my calf breaks, and it starts to bleed again. "Oh, great."

"What?" asks Shawn. He looks at my bloody leg. "Did they get you? What happened?" he inquires.

"Spenser, my deranged lab partner, threw a scalpel at me," I say.

"You should've told me earlier!" Shawn says. "C'mon, let's get you fixed up." We walk towards the store.

"We have no money, and I don't have my bag with me. I have nothing." I realize as Shawn is about to open the door of the convenience store.

"Maybe we could sell something we have to somebody," Shawn says. "I've got my tablet with me. Let's go check out that mini mall over there." He points to a line of stores next to the convenience store we're at. "There could be an electronics store," he says.

"Sure," I agree. "There's bound to be one." We quickly run out of the parking lot of the store and into the drizzle, which has turned into a rain, and over to the sidewalk of the mini mall. Going past the stores, we see there's a book store, and then, Bingo! Electronics store! Shawn approaches it and he opens the door for me.

"Thanks," I say. Inside the building, there is a middle-aged man with gray hair wearing a green t-shirt at the counter. He is reading a newspaper and sipping a cup of coffee bought from the gas station next to this mini mall.

"Uh, excuse me," Shawn says. He doesn't look up.

"Sir?" I ask. He still doesn't look at us. He then spontaneously starts laughing, and then looks up.

"Oh," he says. "Sorry." He takes a sip from his coffee. "Uh, how can I help you?"

"Do you buy electronics?" Shawn asks. The man is now staring back at his paper. "Sir?" he asks.

He jumps back up from his newspaper. "What?" he asks.

"Do you buy electronics?" I ask.

"Yeah," the salesman grumbles. "What do you have?"

"A Fourth-Era Wrester Tablet. Like, the new model they just released last summer," Shawn says, taking the sleek, silver, shiny tablet out from his bag. The salesman stares at it in awe.

"Wow," he says. "What do you want for them?"

"How much will you take?" asks Shawn.

"1,000 merits," says the salesman, examining the tablet. I look at Shawn, and I nod. He pulls me aside.

"Are you thinking what I'm thinking?" Shawn whispers.

"Yeah," I say. "Sell it. We can ditch school."

Shawn and I exit the electronics store snickering to one another. Obviously, the salesman wasn't the sharpest knife in the drawer. You sell a brand new tablet for 1,000 merits, not buy a used one. We walk into the convenience store each having five one hundred merit bills in our pockets.

Inside the store smells like rotten pickles. It's pretty disgusting. "Let's find a first aid kit and get out of here," Shawn says. We purchase a little first aid kit, two small bottles of soda, and then exit the convenience store.

There's a bench outside the store. Shawn sits me down and attempts to help me out with my wound. It's covered in blood, so he first wipes it off with an antiseptic. It makes the wound sting as the alcohol rubs against it. I grit my teeth. "Let me look at it," Shawn says.

"Sure," I say. I then lift my leg up so he can see it. "That Spenser kid got you good." Shawn examines it a bit more. "That looks like it hurts, but I don't think you need stitches for it."

"Now's not the time to worry about stitches," I say. I grab the first aid kid and I take out a large bandage. I start wrapping it around the wound myself.

"Hey. Let me do it," Shawn insists.

"Do you even know what you're doing?" I ask him, still bandaging myself.

"No, I'm just trying to help," he says. I finish wrapping the wound up myself.

"I guess we could try calling home," I tell him, standing up. "I think that there was a pay phone back in the store."

"Pay phone?" he asks, chuckling. "Boy, those are so old-fashioned."

"We don't have our phones with us," I tell him. "It'll have to do. We have some change left over from the stuff we bought. Let's get going." Shawn and I go back to the rotten pickle convenience store. It's now pouring, and the fact that it's cold doesn't help. Shivering, I walk past the counter and make my way to the old-fashioned pay phones in the back.

"Here, you make the call," Shawn tells me, slipping in change and giving me the phone.

"Fine," I say. I take the small black phone, and I dial my house number into it. I hold the phone up to my ear.

Somebody picks up on the other side, but I have a feeling it's not the warm, calm, friendly feeling of my mother. Something tells me that it is somebody else.

"Hi," I whisper into the phone.

There is silence for a moment, and then somebody answers. "Hello. This is Sophia, right? It's nice to meet you."

I want to say something smart-alecky, like "It's nice to meet you too," but the stern and serious tone the person has stops me.

"I'm sorry," I say.

"No need to apologize," the person on the other side butts in.

"Well, did I dial the wrong number?" I ask. *Of course he didn't. He knows your name!*

"No, sweetie, no you didn't. This is your house number," says the person on the other line. Now I'm starting to get really nervous.

"Bad decision you made, making a phone call. That just makes it easier for us to track you and arrest you." There it is again. Somebody who wants me arrested. "That reminds me," he says. "We have a guard on your house. Your parents aren't going anywhere, so don't even think about coming to rescue them. At this very moment, the police force is locating you. We will find you. Transmorgifer."

"Oh, okay," I whisper into the phone.

"So don't resist, otherwise we'll kill your parents as well," he says.

"Sure," I say. The person on the other side hangs up. I look over to Shawn. I don't bother to hide the fact I'm horrified.

"You look like you've just seen a ghost!" exclaims Shawn.

"I might've well have," I say. "They're tracking us right now."

"Who's tracking us?" Shawn asks.

"I'm not sure. Apparently we're Transmorgi-whatevers, and that means we've broken the law. I don't see how we've broken the law," I say.

"Me neither," he says. "C'mon. Let's go. This place smells like rotten cucumbers." I nod slowly, and then I walk out of the store. The weather has cleared up a little bit. It's misty around; however, it looks like the clouds are going to let loose another batch of rain soon.

"Well," I say, "If they're tracking us, then we need to go to a place where they would least expect us. Staying here is a definite no."

Shawn sits down on the sidewalk next to the store. "We could call a cab," he suggests.

"How about we go a few miles from here and find something to keep us occupied and them off guard for a few hours? Then maybe we can find some help," I propose.

"What about our parents?" I almost gag as I remember the person's threat.

"We can figure that out later," I quickly say to Shawn.

"That sounds good enough. Where should we go?"

"I don't know, let's go see what's around," I mumble, and then I head over to a side walk and start walking in a random direction.

"I don't think walking in a random direction is the best idea," Shawn yells to me. He's twenty feet behind me.

I turn around and start walking backwards. "There are a lot of random directions out there," I shout to him. Shawn smirks. Suddenly, I slip on the wet socks I'm wearing and I feel the wind knocked out of me, and I'm on the grass. Shawn runs up to me, laughing.

"Oh, my gosh, did you just trip on something?" he asks. I blush a shade of deep red.

"I guess so. I was going backwards. Will you cut me some slack?"

"What did you trip on?" he asks, helping me up. I turn around and look at the ground. There, rooted in the grass next to the sidewalk, is a sign. It seems to be an advertisement. "CARNIVAL! ONE MILE STRAIGHT AHEAD!" it reads.

I look at Shawn. "I think we may have found a way to throw off our trackers," I say.

~

ANIVERSI

I don't really understand carnivals. They're so incredibly old-fashioned, made before Lochbion even became a country. They serve no purpose except for giving Mutaries jobs and entertaining tiny children. Carnivals are basically distractions from the whole "hard workers for a better future" thing, and it's no surprise they're incredibly rare these days. I remember the last time I was at one was when I was really small.

The carnival is old and rusty. The rides are tiny, and some of them even squeak a bit. There are wads of gum on the street. It's not the best place to hide, but it'll have to do. Shawn and I look around and try to look like we're supposed to be here, but we're not doing a great job at it. Finally, Shawn stops me, and says, "We need to buy tickets and do something. We're going to look suspicious walking around in school uniforms and doing nothing."

"Oh well. Might as well have some fun," I smile. Shawn and I go buy some tickets, and start exploring the carnival in more detail, this time intent on riding rides. It must be strange watching a fourteen and fifteen year old at a carnival.

After almost getting sick on some of the crazy spinning rides, Shawn and I head over to a Ferris wheel. There is basically no line, and the Mutary operating the machine lets us on at once. The Ferris wheel starts moving us.

"So," I ask Shawn, "What was happening when you ran out of the room earlier today?"

"Well, it was just a normal day in math class. You know, graphing cubic functions our tablets. I finished early and stuck my tablet in my bag, and all of the sudden, my buddy James says, 'we're going to turn you in.' A couple of other people had given me threats before, but not any of my friends. It was really weird."

I snicker because it is kind of funny. Shawn's group of minions at school, under normal circumstances, would never do a thing such as that. But this entire situation most definitely is not normal.

"Go ahead," I tell him.

"And so I said, 'What?' and he spat back, 'Transmorgifer.' I'm still not sure what that is," he says.

"Me neither. I've been called that about four or five times today," I tell him.

"So then, the girl next to me says, 'Wow, Shawn, breaking the law again? Too bad I don't have something I can kill you with,'" he explains, shivering at the memory. "I didn't know she could be that violent. Then, I heard you screaming outside and I picked up my bag and ran to get you. Then, James yelled, "Not so fast!" and then the class jumps up and starts chasing me. What happened with you?" he asks. I quickly explain my side of what happened earlier this morning.

"Your story was so much better than mine was," Shawn laughs, and I smile.

ANIVERSI

By now, our three minutes on this ride are up. The attendant slows down the ride, and then lets us off.

I'm just about to ask which ride we should ride next when a girl with strawberry blonde wavy hair calls out, "Hey!" She runs to where we are. Looking closer, I see this girl could be around my age. She has blond highlights in her hair and bright green eyes.

"You!" she calls.

"Uh, hi," I say.

"Your name is Sophia, right?" the girl asks me.

"Yeah," I say reluctantly.

"And, Shawn, right?" she asks, looking at Shawn. He nods.

"In case you didn't already realize, the police is tracking you," she says quietly. "I'm here to help. My name is Emma Amrak."

Even though I don't know this girl, questions roll off my tongue. "What is going on? What did we do wrong? How did we break the law?"

"Shh," she says. "It's okay. I've been through all this before, and it'll make sense soon enough. The less you know, the safer you are."

"But-"

"Trust me. I've been doing this for four years," she says. "First, whenever this happens, which in itself is incredibly rare, they always track down your parents first." I shiver, remembering the phone call from earlier.

"We need to find them," Emma explains. "They normally keep them at your house for a while, so there's no need to worry about that. We get you two to your house as soon as possible. Do you have money?" she asks. Shawn and I laugh.

"Yeah," he says, smiling. "We have money."

"Okay," Emma says. She grabs our hands and drags us over to a cab. "We need to see if we can rescue your parents!"

Chapter 5

~

Policemen

The police are already surrounding their house. So far, there have only been three cars of three guards each, but there will be more soon. They've hijacked their phone-line, being able to use Sophia and Shawn's system without even going in the house. It's strange that their parents haven't noticed the guards yet. But they soon will, and when they do, it won't be pretty. One way or another, it's obvious where the pair will turn up first: their own home. In these cases, they always do.

Oh, of course the attempt at the school was a failure. Brainwashing an entire school is difficult, and for it to sink in and them to actually attack is just plain arduous.

They don't have orders to attack yet. First, they must see if Sophia and Shawn turn up. While waiting, the guards discuss multiple things. There were reports of another person from the National Underground Criminal List at the school. A little thirteen year old girl named Emma.

In an hour, there's going to be five times as many guards, and then they'll be able to eventually storm the house if Shawn and Sophia don't turn up. They'll be able to take the parents hostage one way or another. The siblings just need to show up, and then the real fun begins.

~

Sophia

While in the cab, I continue to grill this new girl, Emma, with questions about what's going on.

"How do you know what's happening to us?" I ask. "What is happening to us?" I hope to get some sort of response out of her.

"You'll find out later. Right now, you're on a need-to-know basis. Sorry about that," she finally gives in, fed up with me bugging her.

"Can't you tell me anything else?" I ask.

"No," she says.

"Please?"

Now Emma's just glaring at me.

The ride to our house is about another twenty miles or so. It is another twenty miles of complete awkwardness and silence after Shawn and I have ditched the idea of asking Emma any more questions.

The landscape outside slowly melts from the outskirts of a crazy, busy city, into blank highways, and back into suburbs. We're quickly approaching Weston, the town I live in during the summer months. I look out of the cab again, and we're two streets away from my house.

"Can you let us off here?" Emma asks. The driver nods, and he slows down to a stop. After Emma pays him, the Mutary drives off without further ado, leaving us all alone.

"Um, Emma," I say. I look at the dwelling right next to us. "This, uh, isn't our house."

"Yeah," says Shawn. "Why'd you drop us off here?"

"Well, your house is near here, right?" Emma asks, striding down the sidewalk. Shawn and I are quick to follow her.

"Yes. It is," I tell her.

"So, if you were sneaking into your house, would you waltz up the front drive after being dropped off by a cab?"

"Why are we sneaking into our house?" Shawn wonders aloud.

"Come on, you two! There's bound to be a police car or two having a stakeout. Use some sense! Is there a back door we can use?"

"Yeah," Shawn says, still sounding confused. He then mouths, *ohh*, as if he finally gets why. Obviously, we don't want to get caught by these guards Emma is telling us about.

We venture along, taking a very odd route home. Emma leads the way. I'm not sure how she knows where we live, and it's probably not a simple explanation either. The three of us end up cutting through our neighbor's lawns, backyards, and we even hop a few fences.

While Shawn and I are a bit afraid others will see us, Emma does it fearlessly; she isn't afraid at all. Soon, we're right in front of my fence in my backyard.

"Is there a gate we could go through?" Emma asks quietly.

"Yeah," Shawn whispers, "Why are we whispering?" Both Emma and I groan in unison. *That's it. Fifteen year old brothers are so oblivious!*

"Do you want to get caught by those police men? I can hear them talking from here!" Emma nudges Shawn in the arm. It reminds me of the way that I nudge him whenever I'm annoyed at him. But we've only known this strange girl for half an hour.

My house is just like all the others in this neighborhood. All of the Sectors have their quirks, and Sector Four's is unity. They like everything to be in unison: the houses, the buildings, almost everything. Just like all of the others, our home is two stories tall. It has cream-colored siding on the top floor, and tan-colored bricks on the bottom. The windows are plain, and the shingles and doors black. The fence is tall, plain, unpainted wood.

Emma steps in front of the gate, and bends down on her knees. She takes the latch and moves it a tiny bit, and it starts to squeak. *Please, please don't notice us,* I pray. Slowly, she opens the latch, and we scramble into our backyard.

As soon as Emma shuts the door, we hear voices outside the gate. The three of us freeze, not even daring to breathe.

"What was that creaking sound?" a male voice says from the outside of our yard. He could open the gate right now, see us, and then our whole mission would crash and burn and fail.

"Quit being paranoid, you weirdo," says a female voice. "Get over here, they're calling us up front for line up. More have arrived." Part of me feels relived that we won't be caught, but I'm let down to hear that more guards have arrived. It's going to make this entirely more difficult.

The three of us quickly glide across the green grass towards our back door. This time, Shawn quickly opens the door, making a "WHOOSH!" sound, and lets us in. As he shuts the door, we breathe a sigh of relief. We're halfway there now.

Almost immediately, I hear the familiar tone of my mother calling from upstairs. "Hello?" she calls. "Is anybody home?"

"Mom!" I yell. We creep up the stairs. Luckily, where the stairs are placed, it doesn't give the police cars out front a chance to see us.

"Shawn? Sophia? Is that you?" My mother comes to the landing. "Aren't you supposed to be at school? Who's that girl you're with?"

"Mrs. Lorain," Emma says. She looks over her shoulder, and back at my mom. "This is a really complicated situation we have here. Could we possibly take it in a room where we couldn't be heard?"

"Sure," my mother says, her eyebrows knitting together. My father then comes, looking confused as well. Mom shoos all of us into the bedroom she shares with my dad and tells us to sit down on the bed. Emma, Shawn, and I park ourselves at the edge of the bed, while my parents stand up. The way we're arranged makes it look like we're in trouble and getting a talking from my parents, not us giving a talk to them.

"Did they do something at school?" my mother asks Emma. "Who are you? Why are there police cars outside? What's going on?" questions emit from her mouth a mile a minute.

"Slow down," Emma replies, cool as a cucumber. She stands up, but she's still about half a foot shorter than them. "I'm dead serious. This is a life-threatening issue. The government is looking for those two. (She points to us) They didn't do anything. They're just in trouble. To get all of you out of this safely, I need all four of you to cooperate with this." Shawn and I nod, but it takes a few moments for my parents to start nodding, though slowly.

"Is this some sort of joke?" asks my father. His brown eyes are peering into Emma's bright green ones. It looks like he's trying to freak her out, but Emma is calm and unshakeable.

"No. If you don't believe me, feel free to go down there and get yourself kidnapped, or worse, even killed. They do stuff like that in these kinds of situations," she says, now peering into his eyes.

"I believe you, but your father and I need to discuss this." My mother looks at Shawn and I like it could be some sort of joke that's going on. She takes my father's hand and drags him back downstairs. Unfortunately, I can't make out what they're saying, though I can hear them whispering. Emma sits back down next to us.

All of the sudden, after a minute of them talking, there is a sharp sound of the front door busting open. My heart sinks. The policemen must be raiding our house, and my parents are downstairs.

My fear becomes a reality when I hear the sound of people crowding the downstairs. The sound of clanking metal tells me these people have guns. I can hear my parents scream in surprise.

"Nrugh!" I croak out. It's a strange mix between a scream, cough, and hiccup. As I listen to what's happening downstairs, adrenaline and fear shoots through my body. Combine this with the feelings of nausea, anxiety, and exhaustion, and I'm about ready to pass out.

"Do you know where your children are?" someone asks. Emma, Shawn and I are frozen rock solid onto my parent's bed. I don't even dare breathe.

My mother must have realized by now that these people are looking for us. Emma is telling the truth. She catches on and says, "At school! Why? What do you want with them? Jeffrey!" she calls my father.

"They're at school!" My father calls back. There is a muffled sound of struggling, which suggests that my parents are being restrained.

Are you sure?" asks the interrogator. "Tell us where they are, or we release the firing squad." My mother then starts bawling. Silent tears fall down my cheek. The self-control I had to show with the death threats I received earlier is nothing compared the self-control I must show now. I want to stand up and sprint downstairs and yell at the people who are trying to hurt my parents.

"Don't go down there!" Emma whispers, barely audible. She must "You're the ones they want! Don't you see your parents are sacrificing themselves for us?"

"I don't know!" my mother pleads from downstairs. Now, I'm standing up, trying to help her, but Emma keeps me restrained.

"Ma'am, you're coming with me."

"No! No! NO!" My mother calls. They force her out of the front door. More sounds suggest my dad is close behind her. Behind us, there is a small window with thin blinds, and I turn around and look through the shades. From what I can make out, they're forcing my parents into a police car. Moments later, the car takes off, leaving Shawn, Emma, and I alone here all by ourselves.

We sit there in silence for a few seconds, staring outside the window some more. It's difficult to tell, but there seems to be 40 or 50 policemen outside our house, patrolling around.

Oh gosh. We're stuck here. And there's nothing we can do about it.

The three of us kind of just sit there. I'm petrified by what just happened, and I'm too scared to do anything else. Obviously, Shawn and Emma are terrified as well. We're trapped. It feels like forever before somebody finally speaks.

"Um, so what do we do now?" Shawn asks. His face is pale, covered in sweat, and filled with terror.

"I'm still figuring that out," Emma whispers. "Um, let's think . . . You two should go to your room and get a backpack or a bag or something of the sort. Stick any money you have at the bottom, and then fill it halfway with clothes. Sneak down into your kitchen and fill the rest of it with food. I'm going to distract the guards, and when the backyard is clear, don't hesitate to go. Trust me. I'll meet you where the cab dropped us off." Promptly, she sneaks out of the room and down the stairs.

"Is she crazy?" I ask Shawn. He looks at me for a second, and then nods.

"Come on. Let's get going," Shawn mumbles. We creep down the hallway to our rooms.

My room is almost empty, except for some clothes in the closet and my bed. Most of the year, I'm at school, but this is where I stay during summer break. With panic and hurry, I yank open the doors to my closet and take out a one-shoulder tan messenger bag. Next, I grab the box I store all of my spare money in, and dump all of the money I have onto the floor. Franticly, I count up 34 merit bills, and stick them in the bottom of my bag.

I swipe random shirts and pants off of hangers, and roll them up tightly and put those in the bag as well. I figure that Emma's going to need some extra clothes as well. She doesn't seem to have any clothes herself, and the stuff she's wearing looks old and worn out. I shove three thin blankets into the bag. Lastly, I take my thin blue winter coat and put it on.

I can hear sounds of quiet footsteps hopping down the stairs. Shawn must be going down, so I hurry up after him. When I enter the kitchen, he's already silently emptying out our cabinets, sticking everything he can into his large bag he has. I join him in this process.

When our bags are full, I zip up the coat I'm wearing, and run over to the closet where our shoes are stored. Although my socks are still wet, I grab a pair of sneakers and put those on anyways. The arches on my feet are hurting really badly from running around without any shoes.

After our silent endeavor of packing, the pair of us creep behind a counter in our kitchen. Hopefully, we can't be seen by the men who are patrolling the backyard through the glass door.

Every half minute or so, Shawn or I take a quick half-millisecond look around the counter to see if the backyard is cleared of guards.

"They're going to the front yard," Shawn whispers. I nod. He looks over again, and the backyard is clear. *It's now or never.* We crouch down and we open the back door. After closing it, we step onto the grassy backyard and quickly, but quietly, make our way towards the gate.

Now comes a dilemma that I hadn't thought of before: should we open the gate and risk making lots of noise, or climb over the fence and risk being seen?

For all I know, there could be guards on the other side of this tall fence that we can't see. Then, neither plan would work. "Just open it," I mouth to Shawn. He nods, and slowly begins to open the gate.

It makes a loud creaking sound, and Shawn and I cringe. He quits the idea of opening it slowly, and he shoves the gate open, magnifying the noise.

Now, we know we're doomed. Although the guards haven't seen us yet, we run.

"What about Emma?" I pant, trying to keep up. It's more difficult now I've got this heavy bag on my shoulder.

"Don't worry about her!" Shawn says. "Run!"

Running? Ughhh. Oh well, I guess It's a bit better now that I'm in sneakers and not socks or dress shoes. Even so, I'm still not sure how I can keep up with Shawn, who's undoubtedly the fastest sprinter in the school.

We make our way through the subdivision, going past houses identical to ours. I hear shouts in the distance, probably the policemen trying to find us. Did they even see us? Or did they just hear the loud creak of the gate?

Next to our neighborhood is a small park, if you could even call it that. It's a slide, two swings, and a bench. Anyway, next to the park looks like the best method of concealment we have to choose from: trees. We could simply disappear within the sparse woods and loose the policemen easily.

"Into the woods," Shawn seems to be thinking the same thing as me, so I nod. The strange thing is that trees aren't very common these days. The radiation set off from the bombs in the most recent World War killed millions of them, and any place on this continent outside this tiny country is too radiated to go.

After sprinting in about twenty yards into the trees, Shawn and I stop for a moment to catch our breath. We look behind ourselves. Most of the guards have spread throughout the neighborhood, and we can hear the sounds of only three or four in the distance. "I think they went into the woods!" one of them shouts.

I look at Shawn, and his eyes are filled with fear. "What do we do?" I mouth.

"I don't know," he whispers back. "Let's keep going, and hope we lose them." We move ahead, not sprinting, but quickly walking.

After a few more minutes, we stop again. This time, we're next to a tiny stream, giggling as it dances by. I kick around a few leaves on the ground and look for any sign of guards. Shawn sits down on the ground, breathing quickly. He looks up in the trees and seems dazed.

It's not long before I see somebody standing about thirty yards away. "Shawn," I whisper. "There's something over there." I point over to where I saw the person.

"Well, if it's not a person, then we're fine," Shawn says.

"Shawn! Sophia!" a familiar voice calls, right where the strange figure was.

"Emma?" Shawn calls back. We run over to the figure in the distance. Luckily enough, it's Emma, and not some guard.

"Where were you?" I ask as we approach her. Now, we can see each other more clearly, and I know that this person is definitely Emma.

"Distracting the guards, what do you think?" she asks. "They're back at your house, still convinced that you two haven't shown up yet."

"I thought they would have the whole neighborhood on lockdown because of us!" Shawn says. "Are you sure they're convinced we're nowhere near our house?"

"Yes. I'm sure," Emma replies.

"That's lucky. How do you know that?" I ask.

"I just do. Don't ask questions," she says. "Now, we need to find a way out of these woods and back into Weston. Do you three know where to go?"

"I think so," I say. "I figure we can just retrace our steps and go back to that little park at the edge of our subdivision. We can take it from there."

"That sounds good," she says. "Let's get going."

Chapter 6

~

Emma

The shock of Sophia and Shawn's parents being taken away hits Emma almost as bad as it hits the pair of siblings. Memories of her past come flooding back to when she was young. When she was being taken away from her parents.

"Emma," her mother sat her nine year old daughter down. "You're dangerous to the world. And mommy doesn't want to get in trouble, so mommy needs Emma to leave."

"Leave? Home? When can I come back?" she asked her mother inquisitively.

"Sweetie, you can't come back. Mommy loves you, but mommy doesn't want to get in trouble. The government says you've been a bad girl," her mother explained to her. "Now, in a few minutes, some people are going to come, and Mommy needs Emma to cooperate."

Tears were streaming down the nine year old's face. "You don't love me?" Emma asked her.

"I do, but Emma, shh. There's going to be nice people coming to help you soon. Please remember I love you so much," her mother said.

"No you don't!!" Emma shrieked. Her mother attempted to hold her back, but she screamed "NO!" and ran out of the room.

~

Sophia

"So, how did you distract the guards? What did you do?" Shawn asks. The three of us have just exited our subdivision, and now we're strolling down the streets of Weston with no specific plan in mind. Our town is like one of those old-style towns with sidewalks and mini-malls on both sides of the two-way street.

"Oh, it's nothing," Emma blushes. She seems to have been thinking about something deeply. "I'll tell you two later. For now, we need to find a place to get dinner and stay the night."

"Should we call another cab?" I ask.

"No, I think we can stay in town for now," she explains.

"Well, aren't they going to have the whole town on lockdown searching for us?" Shawn wonders aloud. "That's what they do with criminals, right?"

"For starters, you guys aren't criminals. Secondly, um, the guards didn't see you two, so they can't be that sure you were actually there. The policemen thought they did, and that's why they followed you. But I can assure you that the town won't go into lockdown," Emma does the favor of giving us the need-to-know details again, leaving me even more confused and yet partially enlightened.

"Anyway, we can just stick with someplace local for dinner. It needs to be inexpensive. We need to stretch those 1,000 merits you somehow obtained."

"I sold my school tablet!" Shawn says, beaming.

"We could always stretch it even more and just eat something we brought from home," I tell them, gesturing to my bag.

"Okay," Emma says. "Cool with me."

The three of us make our way down the lengthy road, looking for some place where we can sit down and eat for a moment. We try to get as far away from our neighborhood as quickly as possible. On our way, we pass by supermarkets with signs advertising discounts and restaurants crowded with people. The sun begins to set in the distance, streaking a rainbow of warm colors in the sky. The clouds seem to have moved along; hopefully, we will get some better weather than we've had today.

"Where are we going?" Shawn asks us. "All of this milling around seems pretty aimless to me."

"Just down the road," Emma tells us.

"No, I mean, in the long term. Are we switching Sectors or something?" he asks.

"If you must know, I'm evacuating you from the country," she whispers.

"What?" I almost scream.

"Quiet down! People will hear us, and we already look suspicious enough. Anyway, let me put it this way: you're one of my kind. You're an outcast because of that. It's illegal, so either you die or you escape. I've helped three other people do this," she explains. *So maybe she really does know what she's doing.*

That clears things up a bit, but I'm still foggy on the whole Transmorgifer thing. "What exactly is a Transmorgifer?" I ask. Emma jerks her head around and looks me straight in the eyes.

"Where did you hear that, Sophia?"

"Well, I've been called that about five times today, and I think it has something to do with all this stuff that's been happening, you know?" I say.

"Tomorrow I'll explain. It must be torture not knowing," she says. *Well, duh. Can't you just tell us now?*

Eventually, we stumble upon a convenience store. Emma goes inside to use the restroom, and Shawn and I sit down by the side of the store. I look in my bag and bring out a box of cheese crackers. Shawn gets a bag of chips.

"Dinner, then," he says, taking the bag, which makes a ripping sound as it opens. The two of us dive in.

As Emma returns, I ask her something that's been bugging me for a while. "How did you know where we live?"

"I do my research," she tells us, a strange grin on her face. I glare at her, non-verbally communicating, *tell us more!* She refuses to budge about anything else.

"That's creepy," Shawn says, breaking the tension. "How can we be sure you're not some sort of stalker?"

"The thing is, you can't," she grins. *That's just great. Way to make me feel a whole lot better about this situation.* After a few more minutes of munching on the food we have, Shawn closes the bag, wipes his hands, and sticks it back in his bag.

"Let's get going," he says.

"Okay," Emma says. "Are there any really cheap places we could stay around here? We should probably use that to our advantage while we can."

"I think there is one that's 40 merits for a room," Shawn mumbles. "But don't you have to have an ID to rent out rooms at a motel?"

"Pfft. What's your point? How do you think I've survived on my own for all of these years?" Emma tells us as she struts forward.

The motel Shawn was talking about is just down the street a little bit. It's old and rusted, painted an ugly orange color. (In my opinion, anyone who paints a building orange deserves a beating.) The lobby is small, and has a little door and two tiny windows on either side.

"We can't get a room here," Shawn says. "At least, not legally." Emma approaches the building and looks at the lobby building closer. It seems that she's is looking at the windows. They're old, rusted, and cracked, but they seem to have some sort of importance to her.

Suddenly, she breathes a sigh of relief. "Good. I think we could sneak into a room," Emma says. "Even if we do get caught, they owner will understand."

"Understand what? That we're 'criminals' running from the law?" I ask, making air quotes over the word "criminals."

"Not exactly," Emma says. She reaches into her pocket, and runs over to a set of staircases leading up to a second floor of rooms. The three of us trudge up the creaky stairs. Emma walks across the balcony to a random room, and we follow her.

She fishes something out of her pocket. It's a paper clip and a bobby pin. She starts jamming the two items into the lock, attempting to open it. The door is probably old enough that she can pick it.

"Is this legal?" I ask.

"No," Emma smiles, as the door clicks open.

"Well, aren't we supposed to be running from the law because we haven't broken it? I think we just threw that whole idea out the window," Shawn says, walking over to a sofa in the room and slumping onto it.

The room isn't that appealing. The beds have sheets the color of mustard, and the carpet is a sickening green. Shawn is sitting on a sofa that's old and gray. I take a look in the bathroom, and there's a small shower and a disgusting sink that looks like it hasn't been cleaned for weeks.

"Okay, if we're going to break into a motel, why couldn't we have picked somewhere nicer?" Shawn asks.

"Because I said so," Emma says.

"Well," I say, poking my head out of the bathroom door. "We probably should unpack only what we need, so we can pick up more easily in the morning. I'm going to take a shower," I say, and I go back into the tiny bathroom.

The shower has extremely hot water, but I'm adjusted to it quickly. As I stand under the steamy water, I wish I could be in here forever and never come out. *Well, it is a hotel. I can take as long as I like.*

"Geez, Sophia! Don't take forever!" Shawn calls after who-knows how long. *So much for taking as long as I like. There's still Shawn and Emma who need to get in here.* After drying off and putting my hair up in a towel, I change into some pajamas I stuck into my messenger bag earlier today. Shivers run through my body as soon as I exit the steamy bathroom.

Shawn and Emma are snacking on some food we brought with us in our bags.

"You took long enough," Shawn says. He scrambles into the bathroom and quickly starts the water.

Emma stays quiet, crunching on cheese crackers. To kill the awkwardness, I decide to go to bed early, despite the time being 7:23 in the evening.

"I'm gonna hit the sack," I mumble. I quickly pull myself under the covers of one of the beds and drift into a light sleep.

~

When I wake up, I don't open my eyes. Instead, I wonder if the traumatizing events of yesterday really happened. As I shift around in the sheets, it feels similar to those in my bunk back at school. *See, look. It feels like your old bed. Why shouldn't it be your bed?*

I then open my eyes and sit up. Of course I'm not in my dorm room at school, and of course the events of the previous day actually did happen.

The clock reads 5:25 A.M. Duh. It's been programmed into my brain to wake up at 5:25. Moments later, Shawn sits up from where he was sleeping on the couch, and he looks over at me. No surprise he's up this early as well. He's been programmed the same way.

`"It's 5:25. Everyone at school is waking up now," I say.

"Should we get Emma up?" I wonder.

"Sure. Might as well get going early," I say. I put my feet on the cold floor and go over to Emma's bed. "Emma. Get up!"

"NGRR!!!" she complains. "Bleh! It's 4 in the morning!"

"No," I tell her. "It's only five thirty. Get up. I want to get an early start to the day. You promised us you'd tell us what all of this buzz is about!"

"Only five thirty? Why are we up this early?"

"At our old school, this is when we get up every day," I say.

"Crazy. Well, we're not at your school, now are we?" she mumbles as she drags herself into the restroom and turns on the water in the shower.

"I was talking with Emma yesterday," Shawn says, "about Mom and Dad." I tense at the subject of our parents.

"Are we ever going to see them again?" I ask him, staring at the ugly-looking floor. I still have hope that Mom and Dad are perfectly fine and we will see them soon.

"Well, she said they're probably gone for good. Emma doesn't know if they're alive or dead or where they've been taken. She does know that we won't see them again," Shawn whispers. I look at him with disbelief. His face is red and it looks like there are tears forming at the edges of his eyes. I exhale slowly as I take in what he said.

Of course, I've thought about what happened to Mom and Dad, but I always thought I'd get to see them again. I'm so frustrated; I take out my anger by chucking pillows at the window of our room. Yes, I know it's strange, but I have a tendency to never ever cry, especially around other people. Even if my brother is the only one in the room, I always find some other way to get out my steam.

I drift into the routine of grabbing a pillow and then throwing it, despite my terrible aim, towards the general area of the window. Soon enough, I run out of pillows and things to throw, so I just collapse on my bed, filled with anger, tension, and fear. A tornado of thoughts and worry run through my head. I can hear Emma singing a cheerful song in the shower, and it almost wants to make me scream at her.

"I'm sorry," I tell Shawn. "I've never been like this before."

"Yeah, you haven't," Shawn says, "but sometimes it's okay to just let it all out."

"Thanks," I mumble. I calm myself down by the time Emma comes out of the shower, dressed in a pair of my pants and a green shirt.

"Whoa! You killed the room!" she says. I guess it does look like that with all the pillows I tossed everywhere. We decide to be kind to the cleaning lady and spent ten minutes picking up the pillows and making sure we have everything into our school bags. Besides, we kind of have to leave no trace that we were there.

Afterwards, the clock reads 6:37. "Let's get going," I say. "I'm still waiting for that explanation you owe us, Emma."

Chapter 7

~

Emma

As little nine-year-old Emma ran, her mother called for her. She sped across her home, out the door, and into the cool darkness of the night. She could hear sounds of her mother calling for her. "EMMA! You come back here right now! You're going to get mommy into trouble."

Does she really think I'm stupid enough to let strangers take me away? *Emma wondered as she ran. Her mother didn't bother to chase after her, which told Emma one thing: her mother didn't care about her. If she really did, she would make sure that Emma would be shipped off with the strangers. Instead, she let Emma run.*

She might as well have yelled to Emma, "At least you're not my problem now!"

Soon enough, she heard sirens wailing behind her in the distance, but that didn't stop her. She kept running and never looked back.

~

Sophia

This morning, Weston is especially quiet. The streets are dark and empty. It's so noiseless you can hear the sidewalk scratching and crackling beneath our feet and birds chirping and singing in the distance. The three of us are silent as we stroll down the street, unsure of where to go.

"I'm still waiting for an explanation," I say, breaking the quietness.

"Just give me a minute," Emma says. *It's been a whole day, Emma. Cut to the chase!* "We want to have fun with the explanation, right?"

"Fun?" Shawn asks, a confused look etched on his face..

"Oh yes," Emma says, excited as ever. "Any deserted parks around? We need to be alone for me to explain." *Way to convince me you're not a serial killer!*

"There's one just down the road," Shawn says, leading the way. A few minutes later, we stumble upon the park, which is basically a fenced off area of trees. They're packed together in tight clumps, and roots and leaves lay scattered on the ground. Immediately, questions start spitting out of my mouth before I can stop it as we hike inside the cluster of trees.

"What is a Transmorgifer? Why are they illegal?" I plead.

"Well, there are a bunch of reasons why they're illegal," Emma answers. "Our government hates oddballs. They want a perfect little country, because they don't want us to end up like the old North America did. They want their perfect little Sectors, and their perfect little citizens. They want conformity. And Transmorgifers don't fall under that standard.

"In addition to that, fifty years ago, there was a large series of murders, and twenty-one people were brutally strangled at different times. Our country was just starting out then, so there was nothing they could do at the time, because they were still getting the police force organized. But anyway, a group of Transmorgifers were framed. When the government found out about their powers, they deemed all Transmorgifers murderers, insane, and a threat to society.

"But the main reason they hunt us down is because they want to do these freaky operations on us and find out what's wrong with us. Being a Transmorgifer has something to do with genetics and mutations, and they think that they can just kidnap us and we can be their lab rats. It's sick," Emma says.

"Okay, so I know why they're hunted, but tell me more about what they are," Shawn begs.

"You're not surprised?" Emma asks, confused.

"After all that's happened to us the past day, this seems normal," I tell her.

"Well, if you're a Transmorgifer, you have the ability to change your physical appearance into something else," she explains to us. "The most common type is what I am; I can change myself to look like another human being. They call us Biomorphs."

"How do you change your appearance?" I ask her. "Maybe Shawn and I are Biomorphs."

"Oh, that's easy. I paint a picture in my mind of what I want to look like. It needs to be detailed and exactly what I want it to be, and then my body quickly morphs to look like that person."

"Let me see. Try morphing into me," I say. Emma stands still in front of me and stares at me, examining me from head to toe. Only a second later, she's growing a few inches taller, and before I know it, right there, standing in front of me . . . is me. Complete with frizzy, dark hair, light skin, and even the clothes I'm wearing.

"See?" Emma says, but she still sounds like herself.

"Ohh, that's creepy," I say, shivering. I stand next to her and poke her, just to make sure that this is real and it's not some strange hallucination. "Try Shawn!" I insist. Emma looks at Shawn for a moment, then she shoots up a few more inches and morphs into him. Now, instead of one, there's two Shawns standing in front of me. I can't even tell the difference between them.

"That's awesome!" Shawn says.

"That's weird," I murmur.

"Does this mean that we're Biomorphs too?" Shawn asks Emma as she shrinks down half a foot and morphs back into herself.

"I don't think so," she says, squinting at us. "But I can tell you're definitely Transmorgifers."

"Okay. Should I try what you just explained a minute ago?" I ask.

"Uh, sure," says Emma. "Just, be careful. Bad stuff could happen if you're not concentrating. Just look at me and paint an image in your mind. Will yourself to appear like me. If it doesn't work, then it doesn't work. We'll move on and try something else."

"Let me try first!" Shawn pleads. He gives ten seconds to clearly examine Emma, and then closes his eyes. His fists clench and he starts shaking.

"Gah!" he says, opening his eyes and looking down at himself. Shawn's still Shawn.

"Sophia, now you try," Emma says. I look at Shawn for about ten seconds, painting the image of his body into my mind. I close my eyes, and I engrave the picture into my brain, trying to will myself to become Shawn. I open my eyes and look down at myself. No Shawn.

"That's okay," Emma says. "Perhaps you're Chlorophists. On the other hand, probably not. Those guys always are tree-huggers. You guys aren't nature freaks, are you?" Emma asks.

"No," I say.

"Well, that's two knocked out of the way. Chlorophists are typically big tree-huggers before they realize they're Chlorophists," she explains. She stops for a moment. "Well, a more rare form is Aniversi. I'm not sure there are any alive at the moment," she frowns, as if she's trying to recollect a lost memory.

"Okay, then, what do Aniversi do?" I ask.

"Aniversi have the power to turn themselves into any form of animal," Emma says. "Maybe you should try it out. I've studied these kinds of things, and I'm ninety-nine percent sure that the putting an image in your mind and concentrating on that picture works for all forms of Transmorgifying. Are there any animals you clearly remember at the moment?" Emma asks.

The first image that comes to mind is the dog that I remember from a day and a half ago. "I think I can try something," I say.

"Make sure it's not too complicated," Emma says. "If it's a little insect, you're probably not going to have the power to turn back."

"Okay," I say. I close my eyes. The image of the dog comes rushing back into my head, and I engrave it into my brain and will myself to become the dog, just as I did a minute ago.

Suddenly, I can feel my skin warming up. My shoulders hunch over and my hands reach the ground. I open my eyes, and Emma and Shawn are three feet taller than me.

ANIVERSI

My heart starts racing and my head pounding as I realize what I am: a dog. Not only am I a dog, I can be every kind of animal I want to be. I am an Aniversi.

"This is so cool!" I yell, but it only comes out as, "BARK! BARK! BARK, BARK!" Shawn cracks up. "I want to turn back now! How do I do that?" I ask, but again, it only comes out as barks.

"Amazing," Emma says, slowly nodding her head. "You must be the only Aniversi alive today. Shawn, chances are you are too. How about you try morphing into the dog that Sophia is?"

"Cool!" Shawn says, like any other 15 year old boy would say. He examines me, still the large dog with brown fur, for a few seconds. He inhales deeply and closes his eyes. Immediately, he starts shrinking, his arms going down on the ground, and his skin turns to fur and he changes into a dog. Shawn is an exact mirror of me.

"Would you mind telling us how to change back?" Shawn barks up at Emma. I frown and I think, *I just understood what he said. He was barking, wasn't he? I can speak Dog too!!*

"You probably want to know how to change back. According to the laws of Transmorgifying, you're supposed to kind of will yourself to change back. It sounds a bit difficult, but trust me, it's as simple as it sounds."

"Okay," I say, which comes out as a joyful "BARK!"

Emma giggles. "That's so cool. You guys are Aniversi!" she says. I take a moment down, and I try to will myself to become myself again, if that makes any sense. Sure enough, after about four and a half seconds of trying, my hands lift up off the ground and I bend back, becoming five feet four again and my normal self.

"Okay, that was the coolest thing ever!" I exclaim. "I could even understand what Shawn was saying in his dog form. It's as if I know the language of the animal I am," I tell Emma.

Shawn takes a bit longer to change back. He takes a few deep breaths, and then closes his eyes. "Shawn, come on," I say. "You can't stay a dog forever!" He growls at me, and continues to try to change back.

Then, ever so slowly, he starts morphing into himself again. The process is slow and takes about two minutes. When he is finally fully human again, he says, "That took forever. I probably should practice."

"That's why I took you two here for the explanation, so you could practice," Emma explains. " You need to be really careful, though. I'm going to tell you the easy way, so you don't have to learn like I did. As I previously mentioned, Transmorgifers are basically genetic mutations, right?"

"Right," Shawn and I nod.

"So, the normal human body isn't supposed to be capable of changing their physical appearance. You've got to be careful not to change too often or into something really drastically different from what you already are, or even stay transmorgified too long. Your body isn't powerful enough to allow your body to do that, so when you will yourself to do that, you'll go on kind of an "overload." The official term is Haywire. Some symptoms are extreme craziness, dizziness and sometimes it knocks you out. If it's really bad, it could even kill you," she warns, a solemn look on her face.

"Wow," I whisper. "Don't want that happening. So, practicing something such as a dog is safe, right?"

"Sure, just to get hold of your powers. But if you were to change into a worm and back over and over again, you'd probably go Haywire," Emma explains.

"I just have one final question, Emma," I tell her. "You were the one in the Principal's office the other day, right?" She gulps and blushes. She doesn't even need to say a thing.

"It all makes sense now," I say. "You were the one yelling to Mr. Nexster in the principal's office. You knew that we were Transmorgifers, right? But that still doesn't explain that strange dog that came into my room . . ."

"The Principal was going to turn you in right there and then. They would kill you, and Shawn later if I didn't do something. I've dedicating myself to protecting Transmorgifers. I couldn't let them torture and kill you and Shawn," she says.

"Thanks," I say. There is a sustained silence.

"But what about that dog?" I ask.

"Um, I don't know," she answers, still blushing. She quickly changes the subject. "Why don't you guys try some other animal that comes to mind?" I look at her suspiciously, but Shawn is eager to try again.

He stands up straight and without even closing his eyes, he starts shrinking until he becomes a large white bird. "SQUAWK!" he says, and I see what could be a smile creep up across his beak.

"Wait for me!" I say, thinking of the first clear image of a bird I have in my mind, and I engrave it in my brain and will myself to become the bird. I then start shrinking as well. When I am fully Transmorgified into the bird, I start squawking as well. "Shawn! I'm going to try flying!" I say.

"You're lucky I waited for you," he says, running away.

My instincts become one with a bird's and I spread my wings and take off effortlessly, as I've been doing this my whole life.

Emma smiles as I soar up into the air. Ten, twenty, thirty feet. I can't explain the feeling. It's as if all of my worries, doubts, fears, and stresses over the past few days have been lifted up off my back.

The feeling of the wind cascade upon my little bird face is the most amazing thing ever. Flying over the trees, I chase Shawn, and he chases me back. We soar above the heavy wooded trees, so high we can see Weston in the distance. After all that's been going on today, I wish I could stay like this forever. I wish I could be a bird for all eternity, and let all my burdens go. Life would be so simple.

Don't stay transformed too long. Suddenly, I recall what Emma said. Quickly, I land down on the ground next to Emma and change back into myself. Moments later, Shawn comes down and morphs back into himself as well.

"You two are naturals!" Emma cries and runs to hug us. "Do you two feel . . . odd at all? You two were up there a real long time. I was afraid you went Haywire."

"I wish you were an Aniversi, Emma. Being up there was the most amazing feeling in the world," I tell her, panting and out of breath.

"I think you two are good with practicing for now," Emma says. "You might overwork yourselves if we practice any longer."

"So Haywire really happens?" Shawn asks, sounding a bit tense.

"Yes. I've actually witnessed it happen before, and let me tell you, it's not pretty," she shudders.

"One more thing! I almost forgot. I should probably tell you about Brainwashing. That's pretty important to a Transmorgifer. Some of us have certain gifts, and the most common one is Brainwashing," Emma explains, changing the subject.

"Brainwashing?" I ask.

"It's kind of self-explanatory," she tells me. "Anyway, if you make eye-contact with somebody and tell them to do something or believe something, they'll do it."

Immediately, Shawn looks into Emma's eyes and says, "Rub my feet."

"Nice try," she says. "It's difficult to Brainwash a Transmorgifer. I guess we can't really practice on each other here, but it's useful to know what you could have. Yesterday, when we were at your house, you two went to pack your bags, and I Transmorgified into a guard. I Brainwashed the other ones into doing what I said. Eventually, I had them convinced that you hadn't even shown up. I tried convincing them you two didn't even exist, but I'm not that good at Brainwashing."

"You said Brainwashing could make people do certain things," I mention, remembering the threats I received. "Perhaps things like threatening to kill somebody?"

"Oh, yeah. That," Emma explains, as if it's completely obvious. "Your school was Brainwashed. I'm not sure how, but the Government has some sort of way they can Brainwash a whole group of people at once when it's an emergency or something like that. I'm guessing your classmates normally aren't so murderous."

"They hated me, but they weren't that violent," I remark.

"And funny enough, even though our classmates wanted to slay us and burn our limbs, *we're* the ones on top of the hypothetical national top criminal list," Shawn notices.

"Which means we're going to have to ditch this place soon enough," Emma tells us, grinning. "The three of us are going to have to evacuate the country!"

Chapter 8

~

Policemen

The police are at the scene of the crime almost immediately after it is reported. It's at an abandoned old park people stopped caring about years ago.

"There's been suspicious activity reported around here. That's all you need to know. Go investigate," says the lieutenant to his subordinates. Immediately, they spread out around the park and begin to comb every little piece of it, looking for some kind of clue. The problem is, they don't know what they're looking for simply because they weren't given enough information.

What they don't know is that the real crime is suspicious activity, yes, but possibly that of the escaped Transmorgifers. Like Emma said to Sophia and Shawn, these situations are complicated. The government can't let everybody in the country know about Transmorgifers. Besides, how can a nation dedicated to "providing hard workers for a better future" get caught hunting down people who get in the way of that mission? Wouldn't that simply ruin the good reputation Lochbion has?

~

Sophia

The three of us show up at our unofficial headquarters: a convenience store. We don't go inside, though, because there are pay phones outside in the back. We've decided to call a cab and get out of Sector Four as soon as possible.

Emma proceeds to call the cab company from a pay phone. Shawn and I stand awkwardly beside her as the phone rings. Something catches my eye while she's talking on the phone. It's a large poster. With my face printed on it.

I take a closer look, and it's not only my face, it's Shawn's too. There is a large, dramatic caption that states "FOURTEEN AND FIFTEEN YEAR OLD MURDERERS." Chills run down my spine as I read what's below our photos.

Great. The government is trying to convince everybody that Shawn and I murdered our parents, and that's why we have to be arrested. My palms start sweating, and a million thoughts swirl around in my head like a tornado.

"Yes, we need a cab," Emma says into the phone. "Why else would I be calling?"

I don't think twice before ripping the poster down and throwing it in the trash.

When Emma hangs up, we grab our bags and move to the front of the store to wait around for the cab to come. Soon enough, the cab comes along, and the Mutary driving it rolls down the window.

"You called?" he asks.

"Yeah," I say. "We need a driver who can take us a long way."

"How far?" he asks.

It would seem suspicious to ask him to take us across the border of Four and Three, so instead, I ask him to take us to a town right next to the border. "Can you get us to Ulnar?"

"Sorry, but I've got a 200 mile limit I can go. I can take you half way," he says.

"Sure," says Shawn. "Good enough."

"Where do you want to stop? I think I can get you to Little Springs," the Mutary says.

"That'll be fine," Shawn says. *No way!* I think. *Little Springs . . . That city is messed up on multiple levels.* But Shawn's already taking out merits to pay and gives it to the driver. Reluctantly, I take our bag and cram into the back seat of the cab. I take out one of the blankets because I know this is going to be a really long ride. *Great. Now it's too late. Little Springs is a strange, strange town.*

"You guys up to this?" Emma says. She's squished in between Shawn and I.

"Well, we have no other choice," Shawn says.

So then the cab takes off. What an exciting way to start our trip to escape the country: A dramatic exit via cab ride!

Since there's nothing for us to do, the three of us have to resort to talking during this trip.

"This is gonna take a while," Shawn says.

"Well, duh," I say. I lean forward and close the window between the backseat and the driver. He probably doesn't want to listen to our weird conversations.

"Emma," I say. "How in the heck did you find us in the first place? How did you know that we were Transmorgifers? We have a while. Care to explain?"

"If I must," she says.

"Yes, you must!" Shawn insists.

"Well, every year or so, I check the birth records of the kids born in our wonderful country," she starts.

"That must be a lot of records," Shawn remarks to himself.

"If you let me continue, I'll explain," she says.

"Look, I don't know everything, but the government has some way of knowing if somebody could be a Transmorgifer. It's confirmed later as the child grows up, but that's beside the point," she says. "Anyway, I guess it's pretty simple. I morph into somebody who works at the place where they keep a bunch of files and birth records, and I go check to see if there's any Transmorgifers listed. Simple enough. I found out where you two lived for when I needed to evacuate you two, and waited for something to happen."

"Fun," Shawn says. "Well, something did happen!"

"Hey, Emma," I ask. "Why were you at the carnival? It seems pretty convenient we ran into you there."

Her face reddens. "Let me be frank. I was there . . . because I love corn dogs. They're my favorite food on the planet, and they always serve them at carnivals."

"Corn dogs?" I ask.

"Yes. I love them, and whoever invented them."

"I think they were made before Lochbion was even around," Shawn thinks.

"I don't care when they were invented. Whoever made them needs to win some sort of award," Emma smiles.

"Corn dogs," I say quietly to myself. *What a lame excuse for showing up at a carnival. Oh well, at least we ran into her.*

Corndogs and secret government business. The only topics the three of us can come up with to talk about during this cab ride.

This is going to be a long ride.

~

By the time we arrive in Little Springs, the sky is getting dark, and the sun is setting. As previously stated, Little Springs is a strange town. Let me explain why.

Parts of the town are packed together in tight rows with flashy buildings like Silana, parts of it are suburbs and streets with boring buildings spaced apart like Weston, and parts of it are just bare fields of grass. To make things even more strange, Little Springs has a reputation of incredibly odd occurrences happening. For instance, part of the town woke up one morning with every building covered in shaving cream. Another person decided to place tiny statues of squirrels all along the streets. Somebody else glued flower petals to a building, and rumor has it they're still here to this day.

Lochbion likes to make itself look like everybody and every town is hard-working and productive, but Little Springs is on the list of the few exceptions. From what I hear, Little Springs used to take the whole hard-worker-better-future thingy too seriously, but that didn't work out too well. Soon enough, it evolved into a jumbled mess of puzzle pieces that call themselves a city.

The cab driver drops us off in the flashy, crazy part of town. Stepping out of the cab makes me dizzy as all the lights come into my view. As my vision focuses, I finally get to experience how strange and odd Little Springs truly is. Neon lights of every single color you could imagine, and even some I've never even dreamed of flash everywhere, illuminating the sky. From what I heard, this part of town would be like Silana, but this is something completely different than what I had imagined.

"So much for 'hard workers for a better future,'" I say as a group of older teenagers pass by, dressed in skimpy outfits carrying bottles of alcohol. Some of them seem to be smoking too.

"Yeah, right," Emma replies, standing there, taking in the city in awe.

"Isn't it strange to know that we could walk half a mile and be in fields of grass, walk another half mile and be in suburbs, and then another half mile and we're back here in the city?"

"Yeah," says Shawn.

"I guess we should get going then," I tell Shawn and Emma.

"Isn't it officially unsafe for us to stay at a hotel?" Shawn asks. "The word is spreading about us. Where do we stay?"

"Shh!" Emma says, and she starts slowly walking down the street. "We can't let anyone hear us."

"Nobody's going to listen anyway," Shawn says. "Everybody is too busy goofing off to notice."

"I guess so," says Emma.

Another thing to add to the list of lame things on this trip: along with dramatic cab rides, our headquarters are convenience stores. So of course, that's where we retreat. (Duh.) Since we're in a large city in Sector Four, there is one just across the street. After entering, we plan what we're going to do next.

"It seems that we always start out in a convenience store," Emma notes as we enter.

"Yeah, I know," Shawn says. The two make eye-contact for a moment, blush, and look away. *What's going on with them?* Shawn and Emma seem to be embarrassed around each other, but they're not very good at hiding it. *Is something happening between them?* I wonder, but I quickly shove the thought out of my mind. *Why would they want me to know in the first place? Shawn would've told me.*

We take the time to use the restroom, get a drink of water, and buy some dinner. I'm sick of surviving on crackers, so I convince Shawn and Emma to let us buy a hot meal. There's a station where you pay a few merits and press a button, and it warms up your choice of a meal in seconds.

After paying for everything, we hang around outside convenience store, eating the meals we bought. I have a chicken and rice soup. It's not the best soup ever, but it will have to do.

The three of us make feeble attempts at small talk, but nothing really works out. In a moment of silence, I notice the small poster behind me. It has blurry pictures of Shawn and I, and it is similar to the one we saw earlier.

"We- we should leave," Emma says, throwing away her container that held soup. Shawn quietly rips down the poster and chucks it into the wastebin.

"Where do we go?" he asks.

"I'm thinking this is going to be an under-the-bridge-highway type of night," Emma says.

"Under the bridge highway?" I ask.

"Yeah. In case you forgot, the three of us are homeless now. But some highways have bridges. And we can sleep under them. Besides, where else can we go? We can't exactly break into someone's house. We can't stay at some building, or a hotel, because we might be caught," Emma explains.

"Darn. I'll have to cancel our reservations at our five-star hotel," Shawn jokes. I glare at him. I prefer to stay somewhere else than under a highway. I'm not too happy about this situation.

"So, let's get going! I've always wanted to do this kind of thing!" he says, trying to throw another joke with a hint of sarcasm out there.

"Ha, you won't be liking it once you experience it," Emma retorts. Emma and I are already ten feet ahead of him.

"Wait a minute, let me catch up!" he says, now twenty feet behind us.

~

Looking for a random place to hide in the multitude of streets and highways of Little Springs is more difficult than I thought it would be. Every time Shawn or I suggest a random place to make camp, Emma shakes her head no and keeps going on. She has a troubled look fixed across her face.

The sun has set, only enhancing the strangeness of Little Springs. Parts of where you look, there's flashing lights, towering buildings, and blinking advertisements. Then you turn around and see a dark night, a few stars, and a large field of tall, wispy grass. Everywhere in the city, the air is frigid and cold. Above, the moon is a tiny crescent.

The three of us roam around on the side of the highway. Cars and trucks race by, only making this journey more difficult. If there wasn't a metal railing at the side of the road, we probably would have been hit by a car or a truck by now. It's difficult looking forward because we're going against the traffic and the lights are shining in our eyes, but we make our way through it anyway. On top of all of that, there is the occasional honk of a car or truck, obviously aimed towards us.

Soon enough, the three of us have hiked around aimlessly for half an hour. I'm about ready to plop down at the next most convenient place we could hide and call it good. It's strange because there has been endless highways and bridges with freeway above and below it this whole time, but none of them have met Emma's satisfaction. After creeping under *another* bridge-highway, I'm about to call camp, but Emma says something before I can.

"Here," she says. "Perfect. We're making camp." *Good.*

"Took long enough," Shawn groans.

"What decides if it's perfect or not? Why weren't the other ones perfect?" I ask, but it's taken as a rhetorical question. The three of us climb up a slant of concrete to an alcove where we organize our stuff. Emma gets the three thin blankets from our bags and passes them around. If the air was cold before, it is a freezer now. I have to bundle myself up in my cover to keep warm. I try to use jacket as a pillow and to block out the sounds of cars rushing by below.

Just as I get settled in, my stomach starts to grumble again. (Like a dying whale, no less.) By the looks on their faces, it's obvious Shawn and Emma heard me despite the sound of rushing traffic below. Even though I had a small cup of soup a while ago, I skipped lunch because we were in the taxi. With Emma and Shawn staring at me strangely, I pull out a box of crackers and start munching on them.

After a few handfuls of the crackers, I crawl back up into a tiny ball with my jacket covering my head. Before I can even think of sleeping, I have to try to drown out the sound of the city and the cars.

I'm drifting in and out of sleep until finally, I awake once more. I'm fed up with trying to get some sleep, so I lie on by side, engulfed in blankets and my jacket. The sound of the city is still there, but this time, I also hear whispering. It's Shawn and Emma. I open my eyes a smidge, and I can see them sitting next to each other under a blanket.

"It looks like I know what I'm doing, but I'm honestly terrified. I've evacuated other people, but the government hasn't been this determined before to find somebody. They never put up posters and stuff like that," Emma says. She looks at Shawn longingly.

"Don't worry, It'll be okay," he reassures her. They stare at each other like they're waiting for something to happen.

What is going on here?

What do you mean? I start a mental conversation with myself. *It's just your brother's love life.*

Love life?

Yeah! He likes her! Isn't it obvious?

It wasn't obvious until thirty seconds ago.

"It's just that one of my missions to get somebody evacuated failed. He was killed. I can't forgive myself for that," Emma says, breaking their awkward silence. She takes his hand, twining her fingers with his, and Shawn doesn't protest. A tiny smile creeps onto his face.

Since when did Shawn and Emma have something? That kind of happened out of nowhere.

Suddenly, a large truck zooms by below us, honking at somebody in front of it. Emma and Shawn look over at it, but then look back at each other.

"I feel as if I've known you for more than thirty-six hours," Shawn whispers.

"Me too," she murmurs. They stare at each other. Emma looks away, blushing.

"It's getting late, and we're not going to get any sleep. I'm going to bed," she yawns, and lets go of his hand.

"Well, aren't you just out of luck? There aren't any beds for us to sleep in without getting caught by the police," Shawn retorts with a grin on his face that screams: *"I'm totally into you!"*

Emma acts as if she didn't hear anything and falls asleep right there, next to him. I turn back over on my side, breathing quickly.

Something is bubbling inside of me, but I don't know what it is. When I look at Shawn and Emma together like that, I guess I feel anger, sadness, or even contempt. But why? Even though they've known each other for less than thirty-six hours, they seem like they like each other.

Maybe this is all just happening so fast, and I don't want Emma to steal Shawn from me . . . No, that's stupid. How could you be so selfish?

It takes me a while to fall back asleep after thinking so deeply, but sure enough, my body is too exhausted to stay awake. I eventually force myself to fall asleep, even though it is light and uncomfortable.

The last thing I'd be expecting is to have dreams. But then again, after all I've gone through in the past 48 hours, of course I'm bound to dream about something.

My first dream is a very odd dream. There are lights flashing everywhere, but these aren't the lights of passing cars and truck from the highway. These are flashing stage lights. Blues, greens, pinks, purples, and yellows. There is also a smoker machine. I seem to be in some sort of party, which is strange, because I'm the exact opposite of a party person .

Although I don't notice them at first, I soon realize there are hundreds of people here with me. However, I don't recognize any of them. Soon enough, after wandering through the crowd, I see faces of my peers from school appear in the crowd.

There's Jennifer, Liz, Ellie, Isabel, and other girls and boys in my Year. I see my deranged lab partner, Spenser, who is awkwardly dancing while holding a scalpel and surgical scissors. Nobody seems to be confused as to why he is dancing with the dissection tools.

Of all people I could see in my dream, I next see Shawn. I wave to him, but he's not responding. I wade through the crowd and try to reach him.

"Shawn!" I call. When I finally reach him, he looks over at me. A frown spreads across his face and he groans.

"Not you!" he says.

"What?" I ask, confused. "You're my brother! You're supposed to like me!" Apparently this isn't the case.

"Blech! Why would I do that? Geez, can't you see? Emma hates you too," he says. Suddenly, I notice Emma standing next to him, with a frown on her face as well.

"Now go away," she barks. *Who am I kidding?* I wonder. *Nobody likes me.*

Suddenly, a slow song starts playing on the stereo.

"Pair up!" calls the Dee-Jay. Shawn and Emma immediately come together like magnets. It makes me feel awkward watching my brother dance with somebody.

It's only moments later when I realize I'm the only one on the dance floor without a date, so I go off to the side, embarrassed. So I watch Emma and Shawn dance. They seem so natural together. Only moments later, the song dies down and my dream changes.

Now, it's complete darkness. It is like this for a minute or two, until a voice starts speaking.

"Hello? Sophia? Can you hear us? We've hacked into your brain to send you a message. This is the government," it says.

What? I think.

"Yes, this is the government. We're currently tracking you. Don't even think about crossing the border of Three and Four, because we'll kill your parents. Be warned."

The darkness turns into a bright, blinding light, and suddenly, I'm awake. The sun has just risen, and it is creeping across the sky. The city is alive as it was last night, because this part of the city never sleeps.

Shawn and Emma are asleep next to each other. multitude of feelings, some of which include anger, loneliness, and confusion, arise inside of me, but I shove it out of my head. I shouldn't be thinking like that. Even if something did happen between them while I didn't notice, I should be happy for them.

My train of thought is interrupted when a loud truck rumbles by, honking, below. Shawn and Emma both jump awake at exactly the same time. They look at each other, and then at me, and they scramble apart, blushing.

"What are you two doing?" I ask. "Is there something going on I missed?"

Now they're both red as bricks. Shawn starts stuttering, like he does when he's put on the spot, and Emma's eyes are wide open in surprise.

"I had a strange dream. The government's tracking us, " Emma tells me, avoiding the question.

"Yeah, I had the same one. But you two still need to explain yourselves," I reply.

"I had one exactly like that," says Shawn, completely ignoring the subject.

"Oh, well. Let's have some breakfast," Emma says, getting three fruit bars out. I know it's no use trying to get anything out of Shawn and Emma now.

While eating our pathetic little breakfasts, the three of us aren't very talkative, so I spend this time reflecting on the first dream I had. *Is it true? Does Shawn really hate me? What about Emma?*

I look at Emma and Shawn, who are sneaking tiny smiles between bites. I'm not supposed to know about the conversation they had last night. Finally, things get entirely too awkward for my liking. I decide to speak up about what I'm thinking.

"Shawn, Emma, do you guys hate me?" I ask. Shawn and Emma look up from their breakfast bars in confusion.

"Why would I hate you?" Shawn asks. *Because your dream-version said so and you're paying more attention to a girl two years younger than you than your own sister.*

"Um, I can't really explain," I say. My mind starts racing as it quickly tries to come up with the right words to say. "I just had this dream last night where both of you said you hated me, and over the past two days . . ."

"Well, my dream self apologizes," Shawn says.

"Yeah, mine too," Emma says.

After we finish our depressing little breakfasts, the three of us decide that we can spend our extra money on a cab to Ulnar. We climb down the alcove under the bridge to the ground, and Emma waves over a cab.

"That'll be 200 merits," the driver says, groaning. She doesn't seem to be up to driving us a couple hundred miles. Shawn takes the bills out of his pocket, and hands them over. We climb into the back and get comfortable. It's going to be another long ride.

~

The Mutary opens the window between the front and backseat. "You kids want to stop at a rest stop at any time?" she asks. We've only been in the cab for half an hour.

"Uh, no. If at all possible, we want to get to Ulnar as soon as possible. Our mother is there, waiting for us," Emma replies.

"Okay," she says. "How long till we get there?" I ask.

"About another hour," She replies.

"Okay. Thanks," I say, shutting the door.

~

An hour later, just as the driver promised, we arrive in Ulnar, which is a big city right on the border of Sectors Three and Four.

"Where do you want me to drop you off?" the driver asks.

"The hospital on fifteenth street," Emma replies. Wow. *She knows what she's doing*, I think.

"Okay. Have a nice day," she says. Looking out the window, I see we're in the middle of the crowded, busy city, and the building outside our door says, "Hospital" on the side. She kicks us out onto the sidewalk. Emma and Shawn volunteer to take our two bags, so we end up in the middle of the busy street. The cab driver goes away, leaving us alone in this huge city.

"Well, let's head to the border," Emma says.

Chapter 9

~

Mutary

The Mutary cab driver pulls into a random parking lot in the crowded city. She sits inside her car for a moment.

Those kids she just drove . . . they seemed suspicious. She had heard about a dangerous gang of teenagers roaming about causing havoc and scaring people, but that couldn't be them, could they? She also heard to notify the police if anybody saw anybody that could be those kids, so she takes out her tiny, plastic phone and dials the number of the police. Seconds later, somebody picks up.

"Hello, this is the emergency hotline, how may I help you?" says somebody on the other line.

"Yes," the cab driver says. "I'm a cab driver, and I just drove a few suspicious-looking customers."

"Can you describe them?" asks the person on the other side.

"Yes, there was a girl with strawberry-blonde hair and green eyes, and a boy and a girl, both with wavy brown hair and blue eyes. They looked like they could be 14 or 15. Also, I heard them say something about passing the border," the Mutary describes.

The person on the other side gasps. "Thank you so much for this notification! We will have them arrested immediately."

~

Sophia

The only way we know we're at the border is because we're near a passing station. There's a two lane road to the right of us and fields of grass to the right of the road. Shawn, Emma, and I are concealed in some trees to the left of the road. Ahead of us is the passing station, which is basically a small booth with a security guard, checking people's IDs as they go through the Sectors.

See, there isn't some big scary wall separating the Sectors, but instead an invisible force field that courses electricity through your body if you do so much as touch it. A thick dark line runs along the ground to show where the force field is, but if it wasn't there, you could walk into the border and not even know. With such tight security, it seems there's absolutely no way we can get out of Four without an ID. I look over at Shawn and Emma.

"We need to make a plan," I tell them.

"Right. They're not going to just let a thirteen, fourteen, and fifteen year old through," Emma says, gazing intently at the passing station.

"Well, what should we do?" I ask.

"Here's what I'm thinking," Shawn explains. "The three of us knock somebody out, someone who's older than eighteen and take their ID. Emma Transmorgifies into them. Next, we can find some car take it to the border. Sophia and I Transmorgify into a small animal, like a cat or whatever and we hide out somewhere in the car. We pass the border with Emma as the person we knocked out, tonight around dinner time."

"That," I say, "Is actually a really great plan."

"Yeah," Emma says. "I was thinking of something along the lines of that. That'll work."

"Is it really that good of a pla?" Shawn asks, proud of himself.

"Yeah. It's relatively simple. Gets the job done," Emma says.

"Emma," I say, looking at her. "Do you know how to drive?"

"Don't ask," she replies, "but I do." She bites her lip, making her story seem even more suspicious. *Oh, well. At least it's one problem out of the way.* Although this plan is the best that we've got, I can feel there might be more problems that arise.

~

I think teenagers whispering in a dark alleyway would seem incredibly suspicious to people passing by. Luckily, since

Ulnar is so huge and crowded, everybody else is too busy to care. Ulnar is similar to Silana, but instead, the buildings are twice the height and the city is twice the area. Being in the smack center of downtown around 4:30 in the afternoon is a perfect opportunity to say, knock someone out.

"So, what do we do?" I ask Emma as we awkwardly stand in the alley waiting for somebody to come.

"Oh, that's easy. We just wait for somebody, and then simply give them a little tap on the head," Emma says, smirking.

"You sound like you do this sort of thing every other day," Shawn remarks.

"Is it really that simple?" I ask.

"See, look, we'll creep up behind, give him or her a little bang on the head, and they'll be out cold. We'll steal their ID and leave them there," Emma explains, fidgeting around with a hard metal rod she found.

"Yeah," Shawn. "I guess when they find out we stole their ID, it won't mean anything to them, because they'll think we can't do anything with it."

A few more minutes pass, and we're still the only ones in the alley.

"Hopefully, somebody will turn up. I think a couple people go through here every hour or so," Emma says.

"Yeah--" I start, but Emma shushes me.

"I think I see someone," she whispers.

Sure enough, there is somebody striding down the alley. Looking closer, I see it is a woman, who looks to be around twenty years old. She seems to be in a hurry, and her shoes are clunking loudly on the pavement.

I look over at Emma. She nods and mouths, *let me*.

Okay, I mouth back.

Emma whispers, "One, two, three."

She then goes out and suddenly gives a small bang to the stranger. It's not forceful enough to kill her, just enough to knock her out for a while. The woman falls to the ground soundlessly. Emma inhales deeply, and she then bends down, searching her purse for her ID.

"She's bound to have it," Emma whispers to herself as she digs through pockets, papers, and makeup.

"Found it!" Emma exclaims, taking out a small plastic card. She squints at the tiny printing on the card. "My name is Maria Wilson, for all those wondering," she says, sticking the card into her pocket.

"Let's get going," Shawn says. "We need to cross as soon as possible, and we still don't have a car."

"Okay," Emma and I agree.

A wave of shiver run through my body as I stare at poor Maria, out cold on the ground.

"What if we get caught?" I wonder aloud.

"We won't," Shawn assures me, smiling. "The plan is perfect, we just need to finish executing it!"

~

Next, the three of us decide to rent out a car, so Emma directs us to the perfect place for three teenagers to do such. It's an old, run down, going-out-of-business-place a few blocks from the alleyway. There's only ten or eleven cars out there, each rusted, and looking like they haven't been used in a while. Emma has already Transmorgified into Maria, and her disguise is perfect.

"Whadya want?" the man behind the counter grumbles as we walk in. He takes a swig from a bottle, and his breath reeks of alcohol.

"We'd like to rent a car," Emma says, disguised as Maria.

"Fine," says the guy behind the counter. He starts talking with Emma about what car he wants to rent.

"The least expensive one," she says.

"For how long?" he asks, gazing at a computer and punching in numbers. Emma looks at Shawn and I for a moment, who are standing a few yards behind her.

"Only one day," she tells him, and looks back across the counter at him.

"Okay, by signing this contract, you understand that after exactly twenty-four hours, your rental car will stop functioning. By then, hopefully, you will have returned it to us. Otherwise, you'll have to pay extra money for it to start working again," the guy behind the counter grumbles, reciting some sort of speech he's supposed to say. "That'll be seventy merits." Emma hands over the money.

I kind of laugh to myself. If this guy wasn't completely wasted, he'd ask for Maria's ID for verification of the transaction. I guess this was the right place to go, because if something goes wrong, this guy operating the place probably won't even remember us.

"Here are the keys. Thank you," he mumbles, handing over a small key to us. Suddenly, he looks at Shawn and frowns.

"I . . . I've seen you somewhere," he yells. "You're that murderer!" Emma corrals us out the door before he can say any more.

"They thought I was a murderer!" Shawn says. I would say something, but I'm speechless. If people on the street are beginning to recognize us, then things are really getting bad. How will we get out of the country? To even escape, we need to cross over into Three, but what happens after that?

The ride to the border is quick and tense, and I spend the entire time becoming more and more anxious about the situation. The outskirts have morphed into grassy fields and trees, and the sun is beginning to set. The wind is blowing, and the temperature is freezing cold. Looking behind us, there's the dauntingly huge city.

"You ready for this, guys?" I ask.

"Heck yeah!" Shawn replies. Since he's the more experienced driver, Shawn's behind the wheel right now. When we get near the border, Emma, who still looks like Maria, switches places with Shawn as he stops the car for a moment.

"What do we do?" I ask Emma.

She frowns. "Try a cat."

After lots of practice, morphing into a random cat is easy enough, so I can feel myself shrinking down in moments. Shawn quickly follows after me.

"You two need to hide somewhere, probably under the seat," Emma says. "Hopefully, we'll be in Sector Three in just a few minutes." She turns back over to the wheel and starts driving down the road.

Shawn and I crawl under her seat. From what I hear, when you pass the border, they check your car manually for people you might be smuggling out. Obviously, they're not going to find two small kittens underneath the driver's seat, and if they do, Emma will probably have some sort of quick explanation, like she always does.

"I'm nervous," I whisper. Surprisingly, Emma's a pretty good driver for a thirteen year old with hardly any experience. Or maybe it could be that we're on a straight road for a short distance. Suddenly, the car stops. We must be at the border. My heart starts beating quickly, sitting there as a tiny kitten under the seat. There's no way this plan can fail, so why do I even need to worry?

"Hello, M'am, how are you today?" the guard asks.

"Doing fine," Emma says, taking out Maria's ID, and handing it over to the guard. They have some sort of conversation, but I don't pick it up. I'm too nervous and my heart is racing. *Stay calm*.

Then comes the car inspection, the toughest and most anxious part of passing the border. too. The doors open, and people start rummaging through the car. All of the sudden, a light shines in my eyes. It seems to be a flashlight. What's happening? I can feel somebody picking me up.

"SHAWN!" I scream, but it comes out as a loud, "MEOW!"

I use my claws and try to scrape at the person picking me up. I'm yanking at him and biting him, and there's blood gushing all over his hands, but he won't let go. Looking around, there's about ten people in the guard's uniform surrounding the car. They already have Emma, who's been turned back into herself, back out of the car, and handcuffed. The guards slam her against the car with force and inject something into her arm.

"EMMA!" I call, but again, it comes out as a "MEOW!" I continue gnawing and clawing at the guard.

"I found the boy! We're going to be rich!" says another guard, taking Shawn out of the car.

Suddenly, I feel something being injected into my arm, and I can feel I'm growing back into myself again. I am handcuffed as well, and shoved against the car. Another needle forces its way into my arm. Shawn's now a human too.

"Shawn!" I yell.

"Sophia!" It's the last thing I hear before my vision becomes fuzzy and everything goes dark.

ANIVERSI

PART TWO: Mt. Dalorn

Chapter 10

~

Camp Takes

The three unconscious bodies are lifted into a helicopter and are taken away. The facility where they're to be taken is contacted: Camp Takes.

"Yes, we've got three of them. It's the ones who've been on the run for a week." The entire police force is rejoicing, for they've finally found the delinquents who've caused so much trouble.

The bodies are lifted onto the roof of the building, sitting smack in the middle of downtown Mt. Dalorn. They are put on gurneys and rolled into separate rooms.

There is no hope for them now because this is Camp Takes: where Transmorgifers go in but never come out.

~

Sophia

Whatever drug they stuck in me seems to be doing the trick. It's just semi-consciousness, simply where I can hear my surroundings, but everything is darkness and I can't wake from it. From what I've heard before, this is what being in a coma is like.

Soon enough, what makes me realize I'm actually conscious is that I can finally think clearly, and I'm not in some sort of black dream-like state. So why the darkness? *You're just tired. You have your eyes closed. Duh. Sleep some more.*

And I'm right. I am completely exhausted, so without even opening my eyes, I turn on my side on this uncomfortable bed-type thing they have me on and fall asleep.

It seems like a long time until my eyes flutter open. After take a moment to examine this strange room. But everything is incredibly bright, and the light burns my eyes. So I shut them again. After a minute or two, I make myself slowly open my eyes again, and they soon adjust to the light.

Once I can see clearly where I am, I take note of my surroundings. I see why the light was burning my eyes so bad. Everything in this room is glossy, white glass. The place itself is only a couple square feet in size. There is a light above me, flickering ever so slightly.

Looking down at myself, I notice how I'm dressed: a white nightgown of sorts. It goes down to my knees. The "bed" I'm lying on turns out not to be a bed at all, but instead a hard, uncomfortable ledge sticking out from the wall. There aren't any blankets or pillows. Instead, part of the ledge is elevated so my head can have somewhere to rest.

Another peculiar aspect of this room is a tiny clear tube coming from the wall, filled with a liquid in a strikingly neon shade of purple. The tube eventually makes its way to my arm, the strange serum entering my body from an IV.

That's strange. I wonder what the purple liquid does. I poke at the IV on my forearm, trying to take the tube out. But suddenly, part of the wall opens, and I quit messing with it promptly. Somebody who looks like a nurse comes in, wearing a white lab coat.

"Sit up," she says. As I do such, the nurse clicks around on a little tablet she has.

First, she bends over, poking at my chin. She examines my cheeks and my face. After this, she looks at the black frizz-ball I call my hair. From what I can judge without a mirror, it's in an ultra-curly mode. I find it unusual that the nurse-lady pulls on one of the curls, and it springs back. Next, she puts my hair behind my ears and looks at those, prodding at my ear lobes. *Well. This is strange.* I want to say something, but I'm speechless because this is just too bizarre.

The nurse straightens up, tapping on her tablet again. "Smile," she says.

"What?" I ask. Did she just ask me to smile?

"Smile!" she says. "Seriously."

"Uh, okay," I say, and smile for half a second for her. *I must be in some mental institution.*

She reaches into her pocket and pulls out a marble. "Take this," she says. I pick it up with my left hand. "Now throw it."

I want to chuck it at her face, but I end up throwing it on the ground instead.

"Good. Do you have allergies? Any at all?" she asks.

"Um, no," I say. I've always been grateful that I never get any allergies, even spring ones.

"Fold your hands like you're praying," the nurse tells me. I do what she says, inter-twining my fingers. She bends over and looks at my thumbs.

"Do this," she says, rolling her tongue. Reluctantly, I copy what she does.

"Is there a . . . purpose for all of this?" I ask her as she taps more on her tablet.

Instead of responding, she shows me her tablet, which has nothing on it except for two circles on the screen: one red, and one green. "What colors are these?" she asks.

Great. Now I'm being treated like a kid in Year A. "Red and green," I say.

"Good," she says. "You're done."

She exits the room, leaving me to contemplate if I really am in a mental institution. A few moments after the nurse leaves, somebody else comes in; it's a man who looks like a doctor. He has a stern look on his face, as if he's sending me hate vibes even though he's never met me before. This man gets right to the point and begins speaking.

"We hear you've been breaking the law," the strange man says quietly. I notice the articulation he uses, and the way he emphasizes certain syllables is like he's slicing a cold knife down my back.

"I'm not sure what I'm doing wrong," I mumble back. I look away from his cold eyes.

Suddenly, there's a jerk and I find myself looking at him again. He's now holding my face and speaks.

"We have your parents captured and they can die at any moment! I don't want any smart-ass comments!" He lets go of my face.

"Okay," I whisper in shock. *Take a chill pill!* I take a moment to collect myself.

"Now, sweety," he says, smiling. He takes a breath before he begins. "We know that you know everything." *Yeah. Mental institution. That's where I am.*

"What kind of everything?" I wonder aloud.

"See, this is what I'm talking about!" He smacks my face with his hard palm, leaving a stinging red mark across my cheek.

"WHAT IS WRONG WITH YOU?" I scream at the top of my lungs.

"You little monster," he snarls at me.

"We know what your little friends are doing. Planning to overthrow Mount Dalorn. When will they realize that we're going to capture all of you and kill all of you?" he asks. He slowly shakes his head and chuckles. What he says reminds me of what Emma told me. *Transmorgifers have been labeled as murderers, insane, and a threat to society. They also hunt us down because they want to do these freaky operations on us and find out what's wrong with us.*

My heart sinks as I realize where I must be: some creepy lab where they try to find out what's wrong with me.

"What do you know?" he roars at me. I feel small and like a speck of dust the way he towers over me.

"About what?" I say, the words coming out of my mouth without realizing so. He closes his eyes and inhales deeply.

"About your little friends. Plots. Conspiracies. Sound familiar?" he asks. I gulp, because I have no clue what he's talking about, but yet again, he's going to interrogate me until I am stretched out thin. *What in the world is going on here??*

I look the man straight in the eyes. I can't believe I have the courage to be doing this. "Sir. I honestly don't know what you're talking about," I say calmly, using every ounce of self-control I have to contain myself.

He's staring over my face. "Are you ready to tell me your plans?" he asks.

I frown, and exhale slowly. I say, "Ugh!" I don't want to admit that I have no clue what he's talking about. He won't listen.

Suddenly, there is a sharp pain in my stomach, and it decides to make a dying whale noise. I can see a little smile appear on this stranger's face as I realize how hungry I am. *I wonder how long I've been here.* My stomach starts making the dying animal noise again, and my face turns red. Now the grumbling has stopped, I start to feel the deep pains of hunger, but I don't dare ask him for food. I know better than that.

"I'm waiting," he says.

"Well, what do you want to know?" I ask. He glares at me.

"Everything that you know about. your kind and what's going on," he replies, his eyes melting my body, and making my knees buckle.

I haven't admitted I know what I am, but I spit it out anyways. "Well, I know that I am a Transmorgifer, where I can change my appearance at will," I say. He shivers at the name, as if it's some sort of taboo.

"Continue," he barks.

"I know that it has something to do with DNA and genes and all that jazz. I know there's different types of Transmorgifer," I force out. The doctor nods.

"Cut to the meat," he says.

"I know that there was something that the Transmorgifers did to annoy the police force of Lochbion a while ago, but I'm not sure what. That's kind of why they've been hunted down all these years," I say. "I know the government is trying to keep quiet about all this."

"Yes," says the doctor. "Anything else?" he asks. His eyebrows lower, and he glares at me.

"I don't know anything else," I say. "I swear."

He continues to glare at me, as if he possibly might believe me, but in reality, I have no clue what I'm saying.

Suddenly, the wall opens up again, the nurse from earlier coming back in. The doctor walks over to her, and they start whispering. Memories of the time when Coach Gime and the nurse were talking flood my mind. How I wish none of this ever happened, and I was just crazy from getting knocked out.

The nurse lady and the doctor.

But all of a sudden, I feel another sting in my arm. I know I'm being knocked out again, and I have to use all of my willpower to stay awake. *You must stay awake!* I know that my consciousness is at his disposal. There's nothing I can do.

Slowly, the world starts getting gray and fuzzy again. The last thing I can see before everything goes black is the sight of the man interrogating me. He has a smug smile on his face, as if to rub in, *You are dirt.*

Just great. I'm slipped back into that subconscious state, where I can't see or feel anything, but I can catch bits of conversation. I can hear the nurse and the doctor conversing.

"What are we going to do with her?" she asks quietly. I listen hard so I can hear her .

Now the interrogator is hardly audible. I catch only two words: "She's intimidated."

"That's the entire point of the interrogation, isn't it?"

"Should we start then, maybe?"

~

This thing they're giving me whacks up my body on a number of levels. I feel awake and asleep, exhausted and energized, and still and moving, all at the same time. The only good thing is that as I become conscious again, I'm thankful I could catch some of the conversation.

My head is already searing in pain, but there's a strange feeling I get in my stomach as I think of those last few words I heard. *She's intimidated. That's the entire point of the interrogation, isn't it?* So they know that there isn't some underground revolution or whatever. There probably won't ever be. Lochbion is doing their job well. Make it look like a utopian society, and secretly take out anybody who goes against it.

Suddenly, an opening appears in the sleek, white wall. A tray is shoved into the room, and on it, two slices of bread and a medium-sized cup of water.

I dash over to where the food is Quickly, I grab a gross, ugly piece of bread and take a small bite. If I haven't had anything to eat for what seems like days, I'd spit the bread out. It tastes like cardboard. *Who cares?* I inhale the first slice of bread, the second one, and then the water.

With remorse, I look down at the tray that was full only minutes ago. I wish I'd eaten more slowly. Now, all I can do is sit and wait. They don't seem to want to knock me out, so that's my only choice. *I wonder what they're going to do with me.*

I wonder what they're doing to Shawn and Emma. Are they interrogating them? Hopefully, they realize it's to intimidate us. Are they torturing them? Do they know anything?

For all I know, they could be dead, but I don't want to think about that. I lie back down on my scrawny, pathetic ledge because my head is pounding harder thinking of that.

I figure I should try to get some sleep to pass the time. My eyes close, but I can't fall asleep. I'm completely exhausted, but not tired at all. It's strange.

Minutes pass. Hours pass. Nothing. My stomach starts to grumble loudly again, but there is nothing I can do to stop it. Although I'm in so much pain, I become tired quickly. How lying on a hard ledge for hours can exhaust someone?

Despite that, I close my eyes and force myself to sleep, even though it is light and shallow because the room I'm in is bright, white, cold, and uncomfortable.

The dream-like state I was in before trumps this by a landslide. I'm hoping maybe somebody could knock me out again, because I'm too much of a nuisance when I'm awake. After a while of drifting in and out of sleep, the wall opens again and I see a new visitor.

Chapter 11

~

Emma

Camp Takes.

Emma knows where she is.

Her scars from last time have faded, but not the memories. She has been extremely anxious for the past ten minutes, but when she tried to yank out the tube dripping the evil serum into her, they put in a drug that paralyzed her.

Then somebody opens the door. It's a man in a white lab coat.

"Emma! It's so nice to have you back!" he says, with a grin on his face.

"Are you going to freak me out and intimidate me this time? There's no underground revolution within the Transmorgifer community," she spits at him.

"No. This time, we can put you right back into the testing. We still haven't found your lucky chromosome! Come on. You know the deal. You know how we work here!" he says, unplugging her from her IV. Almost immediately, she is able to move again. But she knows that the other drug is still in her system.

And just like that, she's lead off to testing.

ANIVERSI

~

The nurse has a tray of food, and a fake smile plastered on her face. The food is the same as yesterday: two small slices of cardboard bread and a plain glass of water.

"Eat up," the nurse says impatiently. "You have three minutes." *Three minutes? That's easy.* I inhale everything on the tray down in less than two.

Once I'm done, the nurse detaches the IV from my arm. *Why do I even need an IV in the first place?* I wonder. She stands me up, and drags me out of the room.

"You need to come with me," she says.

Although it seems suspicious, I don't object. A burst of relief floods through my body. They're taking me out of this stupid room!

The relief promptly leaves my body when I see the hallway. It is almost exactly the same: bright, white, and boring. Exactly like the room I was in, only extended into hallway format. Why should I have ever felt assurance in the first place? I'm still captured in this strange place.

My mind wanders as we make our way down the hallway. Where are we going? Are they done intimidating me? Are they eventually going to let me out of this place? Finally, curiosity gets the better of me.

"Um . . . Where are we going?" I ask the nurse lady.

"We're heading off to the lab for some tests." That is all she says. This makes my mind wander even more. Tests? What kind of tests? Is this like what Emma warned me about?

After the nurse and I trek through identical, monotonous hallways for a few minutes, she finally stops. Our wonderful journey has ended, and now I can know what these tests are that she was talking about. The nurse faces the blank wall, and a scanner pops out from it. She places her hand on it. Moments later, it beeps, and part of the wall opens, with a large room on the other side. The nurse leads me inside.

When the she said lab, I was expecting something like the science lab at my old school. This is something completely different from that idea. Instead, it has ten different alcoves. Each has an operating bed, lots of fancy technology, and blue curtains to separate the different spaces. It kind of looks like a hospital wing in a Healing Center, only there's ten times the technology and ten times the creep factor.

"This doesn't look like a lab." I mumble.

"Quit talking. If you continue to speak and be annoying, you'll have no meals and you'll be put in the starvation chamber," she says. *That's harsh. A starvation chamber? They must be joking.* I decide to keep my mouth shut anyway.

There are nine other people in this lab. Five of them are doctors and nurses. The other four of them have white nightgowns on similar to mine, and have dark, tired circles under their eyes and scraggly hair. These must be other captives. If they look like that, then how do I look? I must look pretty terrible, but I try not to think about it.

The nurse guides me across the room. "Remember," she hisses. "You say a thing unless we tell you to . . . no, let me rephrase that. You do anything unless we tell you to, and you're in the starvation chamber. We'll stick your parents in there too, if needed." My jaw drops. I am speechless. *They have my parents?* Now I know they must be serious about this starvation chamber.

I've figured out that the whole ordeal with the man asking me about "underground business" was to intimidate me. Why didn't they just mention these people also have my parents? That would have made the job so much more easy.

Anyway, I let nurse take me into an alcove and set me down on an operating table. It's no different from the small ledge in my room: cold and uncomfortable. I gaze to my right and left as the nurse sticks in an IV with the strange purple liquid back into my arm. There are two other people lying down to the right and left of me, and the sight of them makes me want to scream and yell. It's Shawn and Emma.

I'm about to call out to them, but I remember my parents and the starvation chamber and stop myself. The nurse glares daggers at me, like she's telepathically telling me, *Don't say anything!*

"Y-You don't have to do this," I creak out, attempting to Brainwash the Nurse.

She doesn't take the bait. "Oh, honey, you're terrible at Brainwashing. I was afraid you'd be like your brother, who almost had me stop the procedure," she says. "But shouldn't you know that your powers are completely useless here? There's a drug running through your bloodstream 24/7 that prevents you from utilizing any of your abilities. Remember what I said earlier about the starvation chamber?" she smiles sardonically. *My parents,* I think. She starts strapping me down to the table, so I can't move. I let her. I can't let them do anything to my parents.

At least I know why nothing works; Brainwashing, Transmorgifying. I've been wondering what that that sickly neon purple liquid that's been attached to me has been doing.

"That reminds me," the nurse smiles. "You need a refill!" She takes a container of the neon fluid and hooks it up to IV attached to my arm. I'm now strapped down and can't move at all. There's nothing I can do now.

After hooking me up, the man who was interrogating me earlier enters the alcove. The nurse shuts the curtains behind him, blocking out my view of Shawn and Emma. The strange man begins to speak immediately. "Where's my manners? You've been here six days and I haven't even introduced myself. My name is Dr. Jacob Ayers."

I make no comment. I don't want to spew hate at his face and get into trouble.

Dr. Ayers decides to poke fun at me. "How are you doing today?" he asks, as if we're two friends out for lunch.

"Take a guess," I spit at him. I attempt to break free of the metal straps, but even trying to move is difficult.

"You seem happy today," he says, smirking at me.

I force a cheesy smile towards Dr. Ayers. "Yeah. You could say that," I tell him. I'm so angry at him I completely forget about my parents and what he could do to them.

"Watch your tone, missy," Dr. Ayers barks at me. His icy gray eyes dig into mine. "You'd better cooperate with what we're doing here, or bad things are going to happen." I bite my lip, hard, trying not to yell awful, horrible things at him. This man is the reason why I hate humans, and why I hate caring about them. Dr. Ayers, the people at my school, they're all a part of the reason. People are just plain cruel to other people. Are they made to be that way? Are they supposed to knock others off the ladder so they can get on top?

As I ponder all the different ways I'd like this man to die, he continues. "Now, we're going to be running some tests on you. Don't worry, they won't hurt at all. If you cooperate with us, you'll be back in your *cell* in no time."

I hate the way that he emphasizes the word cell, as if I'm in a prison. I figure I might as well be.

The nurse pushes a button on the IV machine. A yellow liquid starts mixing in with the purple one, creating an awful brownish color. The mix travels through the tube and into my body. Instantly, a weird feeling starts coursing through me. I feel like I could get sick any moment.

After the huge wave of nausea rushes through me, I start having trouble breathing. The nurse attaches an oxygen tube to my mouth.

"W-w-w-hat are y-y-you . . . Whdaya doin to m-m-e?" I stutter. The thoughts in my head are spinning like a tornado. I attempt to break free of the straps, but I can't move my arms and legs. I'm paralyzed.

"Shh," says the nurse. "It's okay."

No, it's not! I want to scream, but it comes out as a loud wail. Now, my ability to talk is leaving as well.

Now, my entire body is going numb. I feel like I'm floating because I can't feel anything except for the pounding in my head. My vision starts blurring, and there seems to be lights flashing everywhere.

"Wh-wha. . ." I manage to force out.

"Shhhh," says the nurse lady. "Don't worry, you'll be fine," but I can hardly hear her. More lights blind my eyes, but I can't shut them.

I am kept like in this state for a very long time, or at least it seems like a long time. Throughout the entire "test," I feel sedated and out of line with reality. My vision focuses and goes blurry again. I start feeling nauseous again and again.

There's the sound of scraping knives, their noise digging into my ears. Dr. Ayers and the nurse occasionally make small talk, but they could be talking gibberish, for all I know. What in the world are they doing to me? I can't move or say anything. I can't protest.

Then I start drifting in and out of consciousness.

I want it all to end, but it seems like hours before I finally become conscious and stay awake. Dr. Ayers and the nurse stop talking. The scraping noise stops. After an incredibly long time, everything starts clearing up: the nausea, the blurry vision, the flashing lights, and the numbness. I begin to hear properly and see properly.

I try moving my fingers. I can, but even a simple movement like that is exhausting.

The nurse begins speaking. "You're almost done for today." I can hear again. Suddenly, there's a jerk in my arm, and more stinging. She's taken the tube out of my arm. I'm starting to feel dizzy and my vision becomes a little bit foggy again.

"Back to your room now," she says. The nurse helping Dr. Ayers shoves open the curtains, and leads me onto a wheelchair. Thank goodness. I thought they were going to make me walk back to my room! I can't even stand up, much less walk.

Then, I remember: Shawn and Emma are in here too! Over to my right, Shawn lays on a bed, and Emma on a bed to my left. The sight of them scares me. They are looking above, completely dazed, and out of touch with reality. There's the sickly brown fluid running into an IV attached to their arms. But then I notice the thing that scares me the most. Shawn and Emma are covered in tiny stitches. From head to toe, a random design and mess of just stitches. There are tons of lacerations doctors are still stitching up, and it makes me want to scream. There's a scary-looking pool of blood where they are being stitched up. The sick feeling I felt earlier starts to creep back. What have these monsters done to them?

Then comes a loud cry out of my mouth. I begin sobbing. There is a CRASH! as I attempt to stand up and go over to them, but I collapse to the ground. I can't even hold my own weight.

Groaning, the nurse picks me up and plops me on the chair again. She starts pushing me out of the room. It only takes a few seconds for my already feeble voice to go hoarse, but that doesn't stop me from screaming mentally. *SHAWN! EMMA!*

I arrive in my room dazed and heavy-eyed, where I crawl onto my small table that's my bed. I'm too weak and too tired to worry any more. I lay down on my ledge. My stomach grumbles, but I don't care. They've almost killed my brother, Emma, and me. I force myself to drift back into unconsciousness, which, luckily, is easy. I can stop worrying for now.

~

By now, I've come to dread every minute of being awake, because every minute of it is full of pain, whether it's mental or physical. An IV is attached to my arm, with the purple fluid dripping into my body. I want to yank it out, but I know there's no use. Somebody will come in and put it back in. Then they might punish me again.

I examine my chest, arms, and legs. How could I not have noticed it before? They're covered in hundreds of tiny stitches, just like Shawn and Emma were. I spend time running my fingers along their rough surfaces. Dribbles of dried blood are splashed about in random places, but I'm too weak to clean them off.

How am I even alive? I must have lost way too much blood with all these cuts. What were they doing to me? The scary thing is, I've known what they've been doing all along, but I just don't want to admit it.

They were operating on me. These people are using me as some sort of rat in an experiment. It's just like how Emma warned me at the beginning of this awful journey. They think they can just cut me up and do whatever they like as long as they stitch me back together again. Now there's a stabbing pain in my head, like someone has bashed me against a hard wall over and over again.

"Oh geez," I mumble, running my hand through my messy, dirty hair, and rubbing my head.

The wall opens again, and the nurse comes in with a plate of food. It's the usual: two slices of cardboard bread, and a glass of water. "We're going to be running some more tests on you," she says. "You have three minutes."

"More tests? Are you going to slice me up again?" I wish I could say that, but I only say it in my head.

I have no appetite at all whatsoever, but I drink a few sips of water and a few bites of the hard bread anyway. I need the energy to get through another round of these stupid tests. Thinking about them makes me feel like a lab rat even more.

After eating, the nurse takes the IV out of my arm. "Come on, let's get going," she says. She puts me onto a wheelchair. She leads me out of the room and we begin the journey to the lab again.

When we get there, I am led behind a curtain again, only to see Dr. Ayers. He smiles at me, this time a genuine smile. It is something I've never seen from him before. I have a feeling he rarely ever smiles.

"You just might be the solution to our problem," he says, his tone ecstatic.

The nurse straps me down. I don't bother trying to escape because I'm still so drained and exhausted. She plunges the IV into my arm, the neon purple liquid running through the tube. I'm starting to get sick of this stupid drug.

Along with the purple liquid, a red liquid is mixed in to make a dark violet color. As soon as the new mixture goes through the tube and enters my body, my eyes are forced shut. I drift into a subconscious state. I am partially awake, and partially asleep. Thank goodness, I thought I'd have to go through the same process as I did last time, with the nausea and numbness.

It seems like only seconds later when my eyes are forced back open, a frightening, blinding light searing my eyes. The way my body aches tells me that in reality, a large amount of time has passed. When I become stable again, I feel even more exhausted than I did the other day. I could drop dead asleep right now. I can feel my eyes drooping, but my vision starts to clear, and I see Dr. Ayers again. He has a huge smile on his face just like last time I saw him.

I'm shoved into a wheel chair again. They drag me out into the hallway, and start pushing me back to my cell. I actually fall asleep on the wheelchair as I am taken back. This particular test they have done on me has left me completely wiped out.

It seems like only seconds later when whiteness blinds me again. The nurse dumps me into my room, onto my ledge, broken and helpless. I lie down, and bend my legs up and curl into a small ball.

I have never been more grateful for sleep. In this strange place, they've taken away all my freedoms, so now, I view sleep as something luxurious. As they plug the purple liquid back into my arm, I'm too tired to object. I don't care anymore.

~~

Chapter 12

~

Shawn

As Shawn lies on his ledge in his pathetic excuse for a room, he feels completely and utterly exhausted.

But he can't sleep. He's been up for hours, wondering what they've been doing to Sophia. He couldn't tell what was happening to her when they began the sick operation on him. Did they do the same thing to her?

The hundreds of stitches covering his body are also part of the reason why he can't sleep. No matter how he is positioned, his head throbs, his body aches, and the stitches dig into his skin. After a few hours of contemplation, Shawn is forced asleep simply by the extreme exhaustion from the strange operation he was just put through. If he could have anything right now, it wouldn't be more food rations or less testing or more sleep.

If Shawn could have anything in the world right now, he would simply want his sister to be safe from these disgusting operations.

~

Sophia

I am awakened by the sick pain in my body.

That's not the only pain I have. Every moment, I keep wondering what's happening to Shawn and Emma. Are they doing the same things to them? Have they been cut up? Have they been stitched back together again? And what about my parents?

Even though every muscle in my body is aching, and even some muscles I didn't know I had, I pull up my nightgown. Again, I examine the tiny blue stitches all across my lower ribs, upper stomach, arms, and legs. I'm lucky I didn't bleed to death.

After a few more moments, I put my nightgown back down. Suddenly, the door jerks open, and in comes Dr. Ayers.

He's smiling exactly how he did yesterday, a real genuine smile, with excitement gleaming in his eyes. This whole situation is just strange.

"You've done very well these past few weeks," he says. My heart sinks. I've been here a few weeks. How much longer can they keep me here? How much longer can they put use to me before I'm worn out and they have to dispose of me?

The nurse brings me a tray of the usual. The last thing I want is to do something, but the fact my stomach's grumbling makes me sit up. That would normally seem like an easy thing to do, but not for me. Even though I've been sleeping for who-knows-how-long, none of my energy has been restored.

Meanwhile, Dr. Ayers is telling me about how I'm such an amazing patient. "You're the key to unlocking my success!" he beams. I slowly eat the plain tasting bread, mainly zoning out what he says.

"The tests and operations we've performed are going to help the field of science in so many ways," he tells me.

"What do you mean by that?"

"You'll soon find out," he smiles. "Maybe."

Something about the way he smiles irritates me, reminding me that everything I do is solely at his disposal. I wonder how in the world I am helping him. They're just knocking me out, cutting me up, and putting me back together, correct? Yep. Extremely "helpful to the field of science."

"You'll soon be out of here," he promises me, a sly look on his face. "You'll be famous," he promises me.

The snakelike look on his face convinces me otherwise. I'll soon be out of here. Yes. When I'm dead and you guys need to find a place to dump my body. I'll be famous. I'll possibly infamous. Everybody thinks that I killed my parents, and that I'm some sort of criminal. There's nothing I can do about that problem for now.

Dr. Ayers then leaves me to contemplate all the new ways they're going to chop me up. The wall shuts in behind him. I want someone to knock me out, because the pain in my body is starting to creep back again. Most of it has died down, though.

ANIVERSI

A few minutes after Dr. Ayers leaves, a sound comes from the other side of this tiny little room. Ma-wosh! I look up, and I see the hole in the wall has opened again, but nobody comes in. I wait for someone to enter, but after a minute, nobody does.

So I sit there, with an open door five feet away from me. *You could escape.* Thoughts start running through my mind. *You could be free from this torture.* I think. A rush of adrenaline goes through me. *You literally have nothing left to lose.*

I stand up, which is really hard on my fragile self, but the will to escape overpowers it. Quickly, I yank out the stupid tube in my arm and creep out of the room. *They should've caught me by now,* I think. Maybe the security cameras conveniently aren't working. Hey, I'm not complaining. I slowly start down a hallway.

I don't know where I'm going. The halls are incredibly monotonous, and for all I know, I'm going to be caught any moment. Or worse, run into the operating room. To my right, I see a window. I know this will help with my escape. I look out of it, trying to find a way to open it, because I haven't had fresh air in weeks. Looking down, I see a city with streets, buildings, traffic and people. This is odd. Where is this place? I judge myself to be about ten stories off the ground.

I try to look around for maybe a staircase or an elevator. There's bound to be one somewhere. How else would they even get up here?

After wandering around empty hallways for a few minutes, I finally find a staircase. Freedom is the only word that is in my head, and oh how it rings through it. My body feels like it's going to collapse any moment now, but the thought of freedom, the idea that I could escape, it's the only thing that keeps me going.

I trudge down the stairs.

Suddenly, sirens and alarms start wailing, but that doesn't stop me. I don't stop until hands grab me, but even then, I still try to force myself forward. Even when many more hands drag me back upstairs, I still struggle, my weak body erupting in pain. It seems like only seconds and I'm back my room, plopped onto my bed.

I cry out, because the pain is coming back, and it's excruciating. Tears are rolling down my cheeks. My chest feels like it's about to explode even when I do something as simple as breathing, so I keep still and hold my breath, breathing only when I absolutely need to.

I mentally beat myself up. I must be stupid to even attempt to escape. How would they not notice me escaping? My vision focuses, and I see Dr. Ayers.

"We're finished with your tests," he says. A sigh of reliefs goes through my body, but only for a moment. I've forgotten how much it hurts to do that. Then he starts to chuckle. I know my attempted escape will not go unnoticed.

"So that means," he laughs, "We can stick you in the starvation chamber."

There is a sharp pain in my gut. The starvation chamber. "Security!" calls Dr. Ayers. "Bring this child to the starvation chamber!"

Hands grab me again and lead me out of the room, slogging me down the hallway. I think of how freedom was almost in my grasp just a moment ago. And I was stupid enough to take it.

I am dragged down the hallway and shoved into a small, blank, gray room. There is nothing in it. The wall closes, and I think I can hear somebody bolt it shut.

There's nothing I can do about it. Now it's set in stone: I really am going to die.

~~

Chapter 13

~

Shawn

The doors to Shawn's room open, and he jolts awake, having been in a deep sleep. His sense of time has been messed with his entire experience at this strange place.

One of the doctors comes in.

"Hello, Camper 10!" she says.

Shawn doesn't reply.

"Unfortunately, we're finished with your testing," the doctor tells Shawn. His heart leaps for a moment. Does this mean he gets to see Sophia again? "We'll be moving you to the starvation chamber right now."

Starvation chamber? Shawn wonders. "But, I didn't- I didn't do anything," he gulps.

"That's right. Your sister did. We're finished with you now, so if you could come follow me," the doctor said. Behind her, a squad of guards appears.

There's no use trying to escape now. Shawn might as well be dead already.

~

ANIVERSI

Sophia

For a few moments, I just sit there, taking in what just happened. Of course the security cameras were working. It took them only a minute to catch me. How could I have been *so* stupid? I lay down flat on the ground, staring at the ceiling. There's a small air vent up there. Even if I wanted to escape, I wouldn't be able to fit up there.

But then something hits me. How could I have forgotten? I can Transmorgify into an insect and fly up there! Even though my muscles are screaming at me in pain, I calm myself down and imagine myself as a small fly. I close my eyes, ignore the pain, but the shrinking feeling does not come.

I try again, this time determined to concentrate. The shrinking feeling does not come. They must have done something to prevent me from Transmorgifying. Now what can I do? There's no way I can escape now.

A breath in. A breath out. I look around in this cramped room, and I fully realize that this is the last room I'll ever be in.

But then, I find myself screaming. I look down at my hands, and I see that they're bruised and bleeding because I have been punching the wall. My voice cracks, and I become hoarse. I put my hands on my head. *You've done it now.*

My fragile body sinks to the ground. I lie there, staring at the gray ceiling in front of me.

What are they going to do Shawn and Emma? Are they going to kill them for what I have done? Sounds like something these sick people would do.

As if it's cued, a voice comes from the ceiling. I don't know where, but it says, "Because you have tried to escape, we have killed your parents. Camper number 10, Shawn, and Camper number 11, Emma, have been sent to starvation chambers."

I stare forward, zoning out the rest of the message. This isn't imaginable. I am in denial. I don't even bother to do or say anything, because this simply can't be possible.

The voice repeats itself, as if it knows I didn't hear it.

"We have killed your parents. Camper number 9, Emma, and Camper number 10, Shawn, have also been sent to starvation chambers."

Shawn. Emma. Mom. Dad. They're all going to die, and it's because of my rash stupidity. My quick thinking and terrible decisions have left everything I care about dead.

One would expect for me to throw a temper tantrum, but it's physically and emotionally impossible for me, because I'm simply too worn out. But I know that in these last few days of life, I must stay strong, because it's the only thing I have left.

So I simply lay there. I don't have the energy to do anything else. All this testing and operating has left me drained. I spend my time tracing my fingers over the tiny, ugly, blue stitches all over my body. I wonder what my death will be like.

ANIVERSI

At least, I know it will be quick. It won't take long because I'm already so weak and drained, I'm basically half dead.

My throat is slowly becoming more and more dry. I remember back when I had food every twelve hours or so. I never really appreciated the two icky slices of bread, but as time passes and my hunger slowly increases, I would gladly eat them, if offered to me.

I wonder what it would be like to have a glass of something cold. Something icy. Maybe a frosty glass of lemonade. Or maybe . . orange juice. Or maybe a simple glass of water. That would be amazing. I daydream, but it concerns simply water and food. It even progresses to dreaming about the cardboard bread. *It isn't that awful. You just have to force it down, right?*

As I sit and wonder about food, I stare at my fingernails. *Fingernails,* is all I can think before I start gnawing on them. In only moments, every nail is chewed as much as I can possibly chew them, and I have an awkward mouthful of fingernails to deal with. It takes a few moments to get them down, but it comes to show exactly how desperate I am. I have to eat my own fingernails to survive. My stomach stops aching as bad for a minute, but then it begins to ache even more.

I know I have to get my mind off of food, so I force myself to think on other things.

The worst part about the starvation chamber is the fact that I have no clue how long I've been in this room, or even how long I've been in this strange building. Days? Weeks? Months? I've been knocked out way too many times to tell. But that makes me wonder: Is this really happening to me, or is this all a terrible dream? Will I wake up and be in my dorm room?

Well, this is a pretty vivid dream . . . Come on. Of course it's not a dream. Quit kidding with yourself.

Soon enough, I can't think of anything but food. My hunger and thirst begin to increase at an exponential rate. It's terrible, because what I thought was hunger a while ago is now a terrible, sick, stabbing pain. I can feel my stomach curling up from lack of food, and my throat drying up from lack of water.

Hours and hours pass. I give in and lie down, curled up in a small ball next to the wall, trying to sleep. The room is freezing cold, I'm shivering desperately, and the stitches covering my skin itch like crazy. The floor is cold and hard, and the only pillow I have are my hands and the only blanket I have is my thin white nightgown. Despite all of this, I drift into a shallow sleep. How is it that I can fall asleep while starving to death, being dehydrated to death, and almost freezing to death from the cold? I don't know. Maybe it's because if I don't sleep, then I might go crazy. Besides, who knows how long it's been since I last slept?

But then, my eyes open again and I don't feel as tired. I'd like to say I've been in here at least twenty four hours, but you never know, do you? I begin drifting back in and out of sleep, the growling pain in my stomach increasing heavily. Soon enough, the pain is so horrible, I know I'm dying. I know this is it. This is the end of me.

~

So, of course, the last thing I expect is for the door to open.

Something even more unthinkable happens: someone enters.

This is not how it's supposed to go.

I'm supposed to die. I almost want to die. It takes me a moment to realize this person must be from security and have come in to finish me off. I almost want to scream for them to hurry up and kill me, but my voice is hoarse, and I can't speak.

So I close my eyes and wait for some form of death to come. The vicious pain of hunger is still imploding on my stomach, and my throat is as drier than a desert, so hopefully my death will come quickly. Perhaps they have a gun and it will be a quick bullet through the head.

As I wait in silence for a moment, no gunshot rings out. I open my eyes again, they adjust to the person who came in. It's a stranger, dressed in completely black with only their eyes visible.

"Sophia. It'll be okay," the voice that speaks is a quiet, soothing, female one. She gently lifts me up, and lops me on her shoulder. Only then do I realize this person must be here to help me escape from this hellhole. She quietly sits me down on a wheelchair, and starts wheeling me down the hallway. As she rolls me along, she hands me a large bottle of water. "It's a saline solution, but it'll taste just like water."

Before I can control myself, I lift my fragile arms and gulp down the bottle in record time, dripping water all over my face and my body. It is icy cold, but it's so nice and refreshing. *Is this a dream?* It feels real, and I pray it's real.

"What about security?" I whisper as I am rolled into an elevator.

"It's been temporarily disabled. Camp Takes is so lazy with their security. We're getting you out of here. You'll be fine," says the person helping me. In almost seconds, the elevator stops. I am rolled out into a dark, deserted lobby, and then out two front doors. The feeling of cold, refreshing air hits my body. It feels nice.

This is the first time I've been outside for a very long time. I'm quiet as I'm rolled down the sidewalk a few feet. I look at where I am now, and I realize I'm in a city. No, this isn't just any city. I'm right in the middle of Mt. Dalorn, or Sector Six. Before I can get a better look, I am lead into the back of a truck. Someone injects me with a needle, knocking me out instantly.

Chapter 14

~

Gracie and Jessaline

The sisters are woken up in the middle of the night with some great news: some of the campers from Camp Takes have been rescued. They're being brought to the healing center next door. They quickly hop out of bed and rush down to see them.

Of course, the three people that were rescued are unconscious. Of these three campers is somebody they least expected to end up back in Camp Takes: Emma Amrak.

"Why were only three rescued?" Gracie asks one of the nurses tending to Emma. "I thought there would be more than three campers."

"We could only disable security for a short amount of time. Be grateful they are here," the nurse replies. But the nurse has no idea exactly how grateful Jessaline and Gracie are that Emma has been saved.

In fact, Jessaline and Gracie owe their lives to Emma.

~

Sophia

And then I'm awake again. The first thing I notice is that I feel so much better than before. My stomach isn't grumbling, my muscles aren't aching, and I'm not completely exhausted.

The features in this room tell me I must be in a healing center. I'm wearing a pale blue gown, and I'm hooked up to a beeping machine right next to me. I'm lying on a comfortable bed with snowy white sheets. It feels so nice to have a real bed because the last time I've been in one was back in that hotel in Weston.

There is a tube hooked up to the beeping machine with clear liquid going through to my arm. After my recent terrible experiences, my first instinct is to rip the tube out. I have to remind myself that I'm not being completely drugged out by these people. This tube is probably supposed to help me stay alive.

Then it really hits me: I'm alive. I'm not going to die in that starvation chamber! I have never felt more happy to be living. If these people didn't come rescue me, I know that I'd be dead by now.

I make an attempt to sit up. That doesn't work out because my chest starts flaming up in pain, so I lie back down. I take a moment to examine my body, and I find that the ugly stitches have been removed, and now I simply have thin white lines running all over my body. Suddenly, the door opens, and somebody enters. It's Emma.

"Emma! " I cry, but my voice is incredibly hoarse.

"Your voice cracked!" she laughs. She's in her normal clothes, but there is a darkness in her eyes that tells me she's had a hard time recovering. She comes over to me and sits down in a chair next to my bed.

"How are you feeling?" she asks.

"Fine," I reply. "Better than I've felt after all those weird tests they did. How did we get out of there?"

"Well, I escaped, and I sent for help to get you and Shawn out of there," she explains. There's a moment of silence, and then I finally ask what I've been wondering for so long.

"What was that place they took us to?" I ask. Emma groans.

"Don't remind me," she insists, but the pleading look I put on my face is enough for her to give in and tell me.

"Okay, Fine. The official name for the building is Camp Takes. A couple of scientists were wondering what makes Transmorgifers so special, so they decided to kidnap them and run freaky operations on them."

"What did the tests do? I woke up covered in stitches!" I ask. My voice isn't as hoarse now, and it's slowly coming back to me.

"While I don't know the details, I do know that they were taking cell samples from all over your body. Transmorgifers has something to do with genetics, as you already know. I don't know why they had to take samples from all around your body, because each one of your cells has the same DNA. It's a pretty complicated matter."

"Huh. That's pretty confusing," I add. "Dr. Ayers said something about me being their star patient. What was that all about?"

"They've spent many years on this, and have killed about fifty Transmorgifers in the process, so they were ecstatic when they finally found the answer in you. I don't know what this answer was, but it could've been pretty bad if I hadn't rescued you. They would've taken you out of the starvation chamber and done a third test on you. But then once they'd gotten all of the info they needed from you, they would've stuck you back in there to die."

"How do you know this?" I ask her.

"I've been around for a few years doing this sort of stuff. I've picked up bits and pieces here and there," she says, blushing. Before she can go into detail, the door opens again and two people enter.

Emma stands up, and looks at them and nods. She leaves quickly before I can stop her, leaving a lot of my questions unanswered.

"Hi," the two girls say.

"I'm Gracie," the taller one introduces herself.

ANIVERSI

"I'm Jessaline," says the shorter one. Taking a closer look at the two girls, they're most likely sisters, even twins. They both have pale skin and blond hair that goes down to their shoulders with a small Dutch braid running down the side of their hair. They both have foresty, sparkly green eyes.

"Uh, hi," I say. "Who are you?" I ask, trying not to sound rude.

"Our parents own this hospital. You're in Mt. Dalorn, and, actually, about ten blocks away from Camp Takes," Jessaline explains.

"So, you know about that stuff?" I ask.

"Yeah. Our family are Transmorgifers too," they say. They take a seat next to me and start explaining some of the questions Emma didn't answer. I find out that these girls are actually twins. They're Chlorophists, which means that they can change their appearance into plants.

"The Government thinks you're somewhere in Sector Five," Jessaline tells me, "when really, you're hiding right in plain sight! Brainwashing can really come in handy sometimes."

"That's good," I say. "But why in the world do they think Sector Five?" I ask. The sisters shrug.

Jessaline says. "Our parents want us to check up on you."

"Oh. I'm feeling a lot better," I say. "This is definitely preferable to that starvation chamber."

"Oh my gosh, you got put in the starvation chamber?" Jessaline says. She looks over at Gracie, and they frown.

"Um, yeah," I say, wanting to change the subject. I look up at them, and they smile. They stand up, and start walking towards the door.

"We have to go. We'll be around," they say. They then close the door carefully, and I am left by myself.

~

Over the course of the next few days, I slowly begin to come back to normal. The scars all around my body are starting to fade a little bit. They are starting to give me real food, instead of an IV. They're giving me smaller doses of pain medication.

About a week after I am admitted to the hospital, the door opens, a new nurse comes in. She reminds me of the nurse at Camp Takes, except for she's smiling, and she seems more joyful, as everything here at this hospital does.

"How are you doing?" she asks.

"I'm much better," I say.

She smiles. "I'm Shawn's nurse. Are you ready to see your brother?"

"Yes!" I beg. There's no need to unplug an IV from me, because for the first time in weeks, I don't need one. When she helps me up, I'm able to stand and walking is easy. The nurse leads me out of the room, and down the hallway.

ANIVERSI

"Shawn's just over here," she smiles. It's torture walking down this seemingly unending hallway. When we finally arrive at Shawn's room, the nurse opens the door, and she lets me in.

Shawn is sitting on his bed, dressed in jeans and a t-shirt. He looks up, and cries,

"Sophia!" he runs across the room and gives me a big hug. We just stand there for a few moments, hugging. I break apart, and I feel tears streaming down my face. It's a strange feeling, because I've trained myself to never cry, especially in front of other people.

"Shawn! I thought you were going to die!" I tell him, bawling and completely drowning in tears.

"Me? You were the one operated on twice!" he says.

"I'm sorry for getting us into those starvation chambers," I say quietly.

"It's okay," he assures me, and he comes in to hug me again, stroking my hair. "Do you have any clue how we got out of there? When I talked to Emma, she kind of seemed a bit. . . I don't know, touchy on that subject."

"Well, I was thinking. Maybe Emma hasn't been telling us everything. For everything to make sense, she should have to be some sort of advanced Transmorgifer. Like, she can turn into humans and animals."

"Why do you think that?" he asks.

"Well, I guess, the night before we got attacked during class at school, there was this weird dog that was in my dorm.

It was sniffing my tie. Emma already confirmed that she was the person Brainwashing the principal when I went to the principal's office. I think that she was the dog, sniffing my tie, so she'd have a scent and know how to find us."

"That's a really weird idea," he says.

"Well, I guess so," I say. "Well, who else would that dog be? Emma said we were the only Aniversi alive!"

"Well, you know, it could be just a normal dog," he suggests.

"I don't think so," I say, my eyebrows knitting. "A normal dog wouldn't drop 8 stories down, and scuttle away when it saw me." I recall the memory, which seems like it was months ago, rather than weeks ago.

"Would a human do that?" Shawn asks.

"Would a special form of Transmorgifer?" I ask.

"You have a point," he says. He shrugs. "That doesn't matter. All that matters is that we're alive."

"How are we going to escape the country?" I wonder. "We can't stay here forever."

"That's it!" The nurse pipes up. We look over to her. I've forgotten she's still here, probably listening to everything we say. "Jessaline and Gracie want to see the pair of you. They said something about escaping the country and a planecopter, whatever that is."

"Planecopter," I repeat slowly.

"Where are they?" Shawn asks.

"I think they're at their house. It's right next door. Just knock on the front door," she says.

"So we have permission to go?" I ask. They might not want me to leave the hospital.

"Well, not official permission from the higher ups, but I think the okay from me and the request from Jess and Gracie is enough," she shrugs.

"Okay, fine by me," Shawn says. He grabs my hand and drags me out of the room, down the hallway, and to the nearest elevator. He presses the button that says, "Down", and we wait for the elevator to come.

The elevator door opens, and we go inside. I press the button that says "First Floor". After a moment of silence, I ask, "I wonder what a planecopter is."

"Yeah, me too," he says, staring at the door. The door finally opens, and he almost bolts out of the elevator.

"Come on!" he says. I run to catch up to him. We go down the hallway, and out the front door. It's obvious which house is Jessaline's and Gracie's. There's only one home next to the hospital, and it's huge. It could be considered a mansion.

Shawn almost drags me down the sidewalk and through the gate and to the front door. I'm so amazed about how big the house is, and all I want to do is take it in. *Wow. This is incredible.* Jessaline and Gracie must have some other siblings, because four people shouldn't be able to fit into a house that big. I don't get that much time to admire it, though. Shawn pulls me up the steps, and rings the doorbell.

We hear somebody bolt down stairs. No, take that back, it's two pairs of feet coming down the steps. The door opens, and Jessaline and Gracie are smiling at us. "Come on in," they tell us.

The lead us up the stairs to the third floor. Down the hallway, they show us a particularly large room with what I guess is the planecopter. It is basically a small plane. . . with helicopter propellers on top.

"The nurse mentioned that," I say.

"Yeah," says Gracie. "We're going to help you escape the country."

"You are?" Shawn asks.

"Yeah," says Jessaline. "Using the planecopter."

Chapter 15

~

Gracie and Jessaline

"Mom, Dad, we have a proposition to make," Gracie tells their parents.

"Yes?" they reply.

"We want to help out Shawn, Sophia, and Emma. Emma saved our lives, and we will forever be in her debt. We want to take them to Terranary in our Planecopter," Jessaline says.

Their parents look dumbstruck for a moment before they reply.

"Really?"

"Yes. Really. We'll come right back. Come on, we've known how to fly this thing since forever. We've never been able to take it anywhere except Sector Six. You know how much we owe Emma," Gracie says. It's true. Their family owes a lot to Emma.

"Fine," their father says reluctantly. He knows this could go drastically wrong if they were caught.

Gracie and Jessaline jump up and down in excitement and then run over to hug their parents.

"But," their mother interjects, "Make sure you use the invisibility feature. I'll let the leaders in Prudence know you're coming. Go ahead and get Sophia and Shawn. They've just been released."

~

Sophia

"Planecopter," I snicker at the name.

"Well, it basically is a mix between a plane and a helicopter," Jessaline says, gesturing to the planecopter.

"It's still a funny name," I say.

"Okay, let's get to the point," Gracie says. "Because of the favor Emma has done for us, we've decided we're going to take you three to Terranary in our planecopter."

"Where's that?" I ask.

"Terranary is a country across the sea. A place where Transmorgifers are safe."

"Don't worry," Jessaline assures us, smiling. "We've known how to fly this baby since we were six! Gracie and I make awesome co-pilots!"

"So, wait, you've gotten permission from your parents to do this?" Shawn asks.

"It took forever to convince them," Jessaline says. "But yeah. We owe Emma big time, and, well, that planecopter isn't going to do much good just sitting there for the rest of our lives, waiting for something really cool like this to happen."

Well, we're not going anywhere unless we get going!" Gracie says. She leads us over to the planecopter, and hops inside with Jessaline. They press a button that lowers the door so Shawn and I can get in. Emma runs into the room just as we're about to enter the planecopter.

"Come along," Gracie calls to Emma. "We're taking you to Terranary."

"Really?" Emma asks in surprise.

"Yep. Come on!" Jessaline says.

Inside the planecopter is amazing. There are five seats, including the pilot and co-pilot's chairs. In the passenger compartment, everything is a cool shade of gray, with a very relaxing feeling. There are two seats in the front, while there is one seat in the back.

"I call the back!" I say, as I plop down in the back seat. Emma and Shawn shrug, taking the two front seats. The seats are incredibly comfy.

"Can you guys hear us?" Jessaline asks over a speaker.

After a moment of silence, Gracie says, "Well say something!" We then realize that they can hear us.

"Yeah," Emma says.

"Good," they reply in unison.

"We're going to be taking off now," they say. "Ready?"

"Yeah," we say. Honestly, I can't even tell that we are taking off. They do it so seamlessly, if I had known this before I doubted their skills, I would be talking nonsense. These girls really do know what they're doing.

"Emma, why did you have us go hundreds of miles in a stupid taxi when we could just hitch a ride with Jessaline and Gracie?"

"They live in Mt Dalorn," she turns around to tell me. "Right were Camp Takes is."

"Oh," I say.

"I'd like it if you guys didn't get captured by the police, but unfortunately, I knew that you had a pretty good chance of going to Camp Takes. I just didn't tell you guys that," she says.

"Speaking of hitching rides in planecopters, what was the favor you did for Jessaline and Gracie?" Shawn asks.

Emma tenses up, as if this is something she doesn't particularly want to share with us. She gulps.

"You don't have to tell us," Shawn says quickly.

"It's okay," she sighs. "Well, Gracie and Jessaline were kidnapped themselves. I was helping them escape the country."

"You were?" I ask.

"Shh!" Shawn says, eager to hear what Emma is saying. "Let her talk!"

"So, it was a stupid mistake on my part. The Government knew that they were Chlorophists. So we were standing outside a taxi one day. I got in, and they stayed out a few moments to check something in their bags. The next second I looked out of the window, they were gone. Just like that. I freaked out. I was only nine at the time, so I ditched the taxi, and went out to find them, crying." *She must've! That's terrifying for somebody who is nine!*

"I couldn't find them. I had heard of Camp Takes, and I knew that we were only about 100 miles from Mt. Dalorn. It turns out that Jessaline and Gracie went to Camp Takes," Emma explains. She stops talking for a moment. It must be really difficult to bring all these memories back for her.

"Keep going. That's certainly not a favor," Shawn says. Emma rolls her eyes.

"Tell me about it. I was scared out of my mind! Well, back then, the Government didn't throw as much of a fit as they do now when they find Transmorgifers. If we kept our heads down and minded our own business, then, if you were lucky, they'd leave you alone. That's what they did for me, so I used my powers as a Biomorph to get myself into Mt. Dalorn with Jessaline and Gracie's parents. It took me a full month to get to Camp Takes. Back then, they only had Jessaline and Gracie as campers. They were pretty rough on them, and were about to stick them into the starvation chambers to die."

"So you got them out?" I ask.

"Yeah. Their parents were hanging out on the outskirts of Mt. Dalorn, and they were so relieved to see them. They owned a Hospital back in Sector Two, but they wanted to help Campers who got out of Camp Takes, so they bought a hospital and a house three blocks from Camp Takes, and right under their noses, started getting rescued Campers in."

"How many campers have they had so far?" Shawn wonders aloud.

"I think . . ." Emma says, counting on her fingers. "Not including us and Jess and Gracie, I think four."

"Well, that's good," I mumble.

"Wow," Shawn says.

"Now, if you don't mind, I'm going to sleep," Emma says. She closes her eyes, and leans back in her chair. She is asleep in minutes. *Whatever. There's nothing else for you to do, so why don't you sleep some as well?*

It takes a few minutes, and I am almost in a very light sleep when Shawn jumps for a moment. I sit up, and I am almost about to yell at him when I remember that Emma is asleep.

"What the heck was that for?" I hiss at him.

"I found a cooler with drinks in it," he whispers back, pointing at a shelf sticking out from the wall of the planecopter, emitting coldness. There are a few soda bottles in there.

"Feel free to take one," Jessaline whispers from the pilot's quarters over the communication system.

"Thanks," Shawn whispers back. It's obvious he's tying his hardest not to wake Emma.

"Get me one!" I whisper. He hands me a drink, and I slowly open it, trying to make as least amount of noise as possible. As soon as the top is almost off, there is a loud HISSSSS and Emma jolts awake.

"What did I miss?" she asks.

"Drinks?" Shawn ask, handing one to her.

"Thanks," she replies. She then looks behind at me, watching as I finish getting the top off.

"You woke me up," she says.

"Sorry," I smile at her, and then chug my soda. "Where are we?" I ask to nobody, hoping Gracie or Jessaline will hear me.

"About halfway there," Jessaline replies.

"Wow," Shawn says. "We've only been here about two hours."

"Did we mention this thing can go at incredible speeds?" Gracie asks.

"No," I answer.

"Yeah, we've got about another hour," she continues.

"Okay," I reply, and I gulp down the rest of my soda in three seconds. I try to go back to sleep. I don't know how long it takes, or if I'm asleep or not, but Jessaline and Gracie get our attention over the communication system.

"Guys," they say.

"We're having a bit of turbulence. Hang on," Jessaline says, with a stressed voice. I can hear the planecopter zipping around, and I can feel it too. I look over at Emma, she seems confused.

"They're never like this," she says.

"So, you've ridden in this before?" I ask.

"Yeah. When I was nine. They took me out a few miles four years ago," Emma says, gripping her chair. We suddenly hear Gracie over the communication system again.

"Guys. . . I think we may-" but she is cut off.

"We may what?" Shawn asks. Now, we're all moving around in our seats. It seems like we're being jerked around in one of those rides in that carnival we went to. Then suddenly, I feel gravity take in, and I realize that we are falling.

"What?" Emma yells. She forces herself up, which is pretty hard when you're in a falling vehicle, and she goes over to the door of the pilot's compartment. "Gracie! Jessaline!" she calls, trying to wrench the door open.

"Emma!" I bellow, but the next thing that happens is there is a loud CRASH! and the plane copter erupts into flames.

~

The bright orange flames engulf the plane, and it's the only thing I can see. I could be in an oven for all I know because the flames are inching closer. *I need to save myself.*

Wait, what? No. What about Shawn? What about Emma or Gracie or Jessaline? Gracie and Jessaline are the reason we're even out of Lochbion and into Terranary.

ANIVERSI

"Shawn!" I call out, but I can't hear any reply. A sudden path in the flames opens, and I run through the charred plane. The metal is so brittle and weak from the fire that I am able to break a hole in the copter. I look around, and I see that Shawn and Emma are already out of the planecopter.

"Gracie!" I yell. "Jessaline!"

There is no reply. I turn to Shawn and Emma. "Are they already out here?" I ask.

"No," Emma replies. It looks like she's on the verge of tears. She tries to run back over to the flames, and Shawn restrains her before she can catch hurt herself.

"Don't," he yells.

"We've already lost Jessaline and Gracie, and I don't need to lose you too!" he pleads. Then, Emma breaks into tears, and circles the edge of the still flaming planecopter, trying to see if they've escaped somehow, but she's unsuccessful.

"What am I going to say to their parents?" she pleads. "Oh yeah, we kind of crashed, and Gracie and Jessaline kind of died?" she continues sobbing.

"Emma," Shawn says, staring at the pilot's compartment, which is hardly even a pilot's compartment. The plane has been burned so badly, it's starting to collapse, and fire is the only thing you can see in the copter. "I don't think. . ." but he chokes a sob and doesn't continue.

With Emma's state, there's no use trying to help her. It's just one of those times where you have to let them mourn.

Emma's now on her knees, sobbing what seems to be buckets of tears.

"They've. . ." she manages. "They've done so much for us and then they. . . They're not like this. They don't crash."

She must be going crazy, because she then starts speaking gibberish. "Remind me. I need to track down Shawn and Sophia! I think they're Transmorgifers. Also, there's a carnival in town, and that means corndogs! Save your money so you can get one! The principal suspects them . . . Also, remember to turn into a dog so you can go get Sophia's scent-"

She is cut off by Shawn shaking her. "You're an Aniversi?" he asks.

She stares at him, "No, it's just, the last time I was at Takes, they did an operation wrong. I have Biomorph and Aniversi powers," she says in a haze. So that explains what that mysterious dog was doing the night before I escaped. It was Emma, getting my scent so she could track me down.

She then snaps back into reality. "Did I really just tell you guys that?" she groans.

"Why didn't you in the first place?" I say.

"No time for this now," she says, staring at the flames, which are slowly dying down. She wipes a tear from her face.

"C'mon," she says. "We're just outside the town we were going to land in. Prudence"

"How do you know where to go?" I ask, as she grabs Shawn and my hand, and drags us down the hill full of dead grass. Up ahead, about two miles, is a wall, and behind it, is a thriving city.

It's two miles of walking to get to the city, and they go by very quickly. I soon find myself facing a fifteen feet tall solid steel wall. Actually, taking a closer look at this wall, it seems to not be closing the people from the outside, but instead closing the outside from the people. It's like the wall is meant to keep out wild animals, instead of keeping in the people. This little fact calms me down a little bit.

Up in a tower is a guard, who takes a minute to come down to where we are. He has a quick, hushed conversation with Emma, but I am too traumatized from the recent events to notice what they're saying.

I only pay attention to the last little bit, where he holds out a shard of glass, and Emma nods, smiling. "Thanks," she says, and he climbs back up into his tower, and suddenly, a part of the wall opens, and Emma drags Shawn and I through the wall. On the other side of the wall, there is more than a thriving city. It looks to be like some huge capital for a country, which it probably is.

"Welcome to the capitol of Terranary. Prudence," Emma says.

"Prudence?" Shawn asks, and Emma nods.

"Come on. I say we meet with the country officials right now," Emma says. Country officials? But, wait, why?

Before I even realize it, Emma leads the way down busy streets, cheerful and full of life. It's weird for me, not being wanted by the officials of the country, and constantly looking over my back to see if I'm being followed. It gives me a sense of security. Maybe this place isn't terrible. We're standing outside of a large, ten story building. Emma leads us to the glass door, and taped to the door is a shard of glass, the second I've seen today.

"Remind me to ask Emma what that shard of glass means," I whisper to Shawn as we enter the building.

"Yeah, I was wondering that myself," he replies. Emma walks up to the person behind the counter in the lobby.

"I need a meeting with the President," she says.

"Why?" says the lady, who is looking over her glasses.

Emma points to the shard of glass on the door. "Because of that," she says.

The lady jolts and says, "I thought there were five of you?"

"Were," Emma retorts snarkily. The lady presses a button and an elevator door opens.

"They'll be right with you. Tenth floor, room 119," she says.

The elevator is painstakingly quiet. Although there are tons of questions revolving around my head, I don't bother to ask them because Emma is still silently weeping for Jessaline and Gracie. Part of me wants to believe they could still be alive, but nobody could survive the fire that was in the pilot's chambers. Even I have to embrace the fact that they are dead, or currently dying from injuries.

I look back over at Emma and I see Shawn's hugging her. It's all I can do not to roll my eyes. Fine. Just face it. They like each other. It's not that hard to take in, seeing that they've seemed that way since we were under that highway a few weeks ago.

The door finally opens, and I see a sign that says, "Rooms 100-119 this way," with an arrow pointing to the right. And "Rooms 120-139 this way," with an arrow pointing left.

"I believe we go right," I say. Once we reach room 119, Emma knocks, and a stern voice tells us to enter.

She opens the heavy door, and there seems to be some sort of meeting about to start, with three empty chairs. We stand there for a moment before the same voice, who is at the head of the table says,

"Sit down, please." Emma takes the chair opposite from the man with the stern voice. I guess this is the president person we're meeting with. I take a seat to the right of Emma, and Shawn to the left.

"I am the president of Terranary. You can call me Commander Carvenaw," he tells us.

Silence.

"You three are Transmorgifers, correct?" he asks.

"Yes," we all say.

"What kind?" he asks not us, but the person to his left.

"I'm a Biomorph, and these two are Aniversi," Emma says.

There's a gasp from the room. People whisper to each other, *two Aniversi?*

Commander Carvenaw shushes the room, and it goes silent almost at once. He slips out a shard of glass for the third time today, and sets it on the table. The room is silent, so I ask, "What does that shard of glass mean? That's the third time I've seen it today!"

"It's a secret symbol," replies the Commander. "It basically means, 'Transmorgifers are safe here.'" That explains a lot.

"We thought you knew," says the lady beside the Commander.

Emma gains a sudden interest in her shoes and turns red. "Sorry," she mumbles. "Forgot about that."

"That's alright, she knows now," Commander Carvenaw says.

"Let's get to the point. This patch of glass here, the symbol that you are safe, this goes for all of Terranary. All Transmorgifers are safe here, because we believe they're ordinary people with extraordinary powers," he says. I take a sigh of relief. I am counted as human here, and not some test monkey. He continues,

"Recent Censuses tell us that there are four other Transmorgifers living here in Terranary. We've also found that all the Transmorgifers currently living in Terranary have successfully been captured by Camp Takes." Camp Takes. I shudder at the name, as the terrible memories flood back into my mind.

"They can't be rescued?" Emma asks.

"That's what the three of you are here for," he says. "Extraordinary rescue missions calls for extraordinary powers." It takes a moment for me to realize that he wants me to go back into Lochbion.

"You . . . want us to go back?" Shawn stutters.

"What?" I ask. "We almost died in there, and two of us died getting out!" Emma glares at me, and I can see she's holding back tears.

"Here's what we're going to do," he says. "We take you back to Mt. Dalorn in one of our pods. You break into Camp Takes, and rescue the campers there. For good measure, it would also be nice to delete all the files they've made over the past twenty years the camp has been open. The camp will have nobody to work on, and no files to study. The camp will have to shut down."

The choice tears me apart. How can I refuse this offer? But I will have to go back into Lochbion, back into Camp Takes, my *favorite* place in the world. If I ever feel like being cut open and operated on to "Further the field of science."

"Let's do it," I say.

~~

Chapter 16

~

Lochbion's Embassy

The head of security for Lochbion is trembling. He's facing outside the Embassy's meeting room. They've called him so he can give them an update on security.

As he paces back in forth, he knows he's going to be in trouble. If he stays back and doesn't give them the bad news, he'll get fired. If he comes and ends up giving the bad news, he'll still probably get fired.

It's a dark room with ten people having a meeting, surrounding a large rectangular table. "Your daily update, Willis," calls the woman with the evil stare at the head of the table. This is the head of the Embassy; his boss. The person who's about to fire him any moment.

"You know of the three Transmorgifers who've caused us lots of trouble?" the man trembles.

"Yes, of course I know of them!" she barks back. Everybody's staring at poor Willis now. Their glares make it even worse.

"Um, well, they've escaped Camp Takes. Their whereabouts are unknown," he creaks out.

"WHEN WAS THIS?" roars the head of the Embassy. "This is awful! Why didn't you stop them?"

"They escaped about three weeks ago," Willis creaks out.

"YOU'RE FIRED!"

~

Sophia

"What?" Shawn yells. "No we won't!"

"Yes we will!" I say, now sure of it.

"Emma! What do you think?" Shawn asks. Emma's spacing out, looking at the floor.

"But. . . what if we fail? What if they over-power us and capture us again? I don't want to go back to that awful, pathetic place for a third time!" she protests.

"You . . . most likely won't fail," Commander Carvenaw says. "Although Camp Takes has some of the best security in the world, you got out twice before, right, Emma? Who says you can't do it again?"

"And besides," he continues. "We'll put you three in a two-week intensive training session at Ivandale Hall, where the best agents in the country train. With the training, the weapons, and the help we give you, and the fact you three are Transmorgifers, there's almost no way you can fail."

"Yes, notice the 'almost' in that statement," Emma murmurs.

ANIVERSI

I look at Shawn and her, desperate for some answers. If they don't agree to this mission, I might have to do it by myself. Finally, after a few tense moments of silence, Shawn speaks up.

"Fine," he declares. "We'll do it." The look on Emma's face suggests she's still not convinced.

"By doing this, you can shut down the camp completely. They'll have nobody to test on, and no files to study. They'll have to stop business altogether," Carvenaw says.

"I . . . I just don't want to throw Gracie and Jessaline's favor completely out the window. They brought us here and died in the process. To risk our lives again wouldn't be right," Emma says. She bites her lip, and digs her hand in her pockets.

"You remember that shard of glass in the window downstairs, correct?" a lady to the right of me says. "You three are safe here. We want even more people to be safe. Remember, we'll enroll you three in the best agent training facility in the country. There's almost no way this can go wrong."

"There you go again, using shallow words such as 'almost,'" Emma grumbles sarcastically. She looks up from the ground and glares daggers into the faces of Terranary's Embassy. Her face is pale, her palms clammy, and you can see specks of tears in the corners of her eyes. "I *hate* that country," she growls. She says *that country* almost as if the word "Lochbion" is a curse word. "Do you realize what they've done to me?" she yells. "My parents kicked me out of the house when I was nine because the government found out what I was, and they didn't want to get in trouble. I got shipped off to Camp Takes once when I was ten and more recently, again now that I'm thirteen. THEY'VE MADE MY LIFE HELL AND NOW YOU WANT ME TO GO BACK THERE?" Now she's standing up. Her face is covered in tears and she's filled with rage and anger.

An embassy member cuts in. "Emma, we understan-"

"NO. YOU DON'T. Have you been cut up into shreds twice just so some stupid doctors could find out what's wrong with you? Have you been on your own for four years of your life, homeless? YOU DON'T KNOW," she roars, and then she dashes out of the room. Guards immediately chase after her.

"Emma!" I call, but it's too late. Immediately, Shawn stands up and speeds out of the room, going after the guards and Emma. I'm about to chase after him when an Embassy member stops me.

"Sophia, if you will let us, we can send you to Ivandale Hall for a tour. Shawn and Emma will catch up with you in a while," the person says.

"All right," I say. I bite my lip. "Just have them hurry up."

"Certainly," she replies. "Hand this to the person at the front desk at Ivandale." The woman hands me a flat shard of glass, the one I've been seeing around a lot recently. "Careful not to cut yourself," she smiles.

ANIVERSI

I take the shard of glass, wondering why I would need it. Perhaps it has something to do with Transmorgifers.

One of their guards (their supply seems endless) escorts me back downstairs, and into a small black car. As I step into the car, the guard comes in as well and sits next to me. "Where is this taking us?" I wonder aloud.

"Ivandale Hall. It's the best secret agent base on the planet. It's a little bit of a ride," he replies. The windows darken, completely obscuring my view of the outside.

"Why the darkened windows?" I ask.

"It's a spy base; obviously, we don't want people knowing where it is. I don't even know where it is, and yet I trained there for two years a while back," the guard grunts.

"Oh," I say. "Okay." *I wonder what's going on with Shawn and Emma. Was it the right idea to ask them to do this? Emma's been through so much.* But then I remember the hopelessness I felt while in Camp Takes. I gave up on life altogether, and when I was shut in that awful chamber, I was fully prepared for death with no hope leftover. I remember how awful it was to have the worth and dignity drained from me in almost an instant.

I rub my arm, full of tiny white scars, and my stomach tightens. I don't want to reminisce upon this.

But I can't stop thinking about how there must be some other campers there, right at this moment. I want to help them escape and give them another chance at life. As I wonder, I realize how selfish I used to be, before this terrifying journey, and how I would only think of myself. But now I'm volunteering, and I'm almost excited to save the campers and shut down business.

I contemplate this and many other things for the twenty or thirty minutes I'm stuck in this dark car. The driver and the guard don't speak the whole way there.

Finally, after who-knows-how-long, the windows start to clear up. Looking outside of them, I see we're in a parking garage. The driver opens the door and leads the guard and I out. The guard escorts me to a door ten feet away from the car, and leads me into this "Ivandale Hall" everybody's been talking about. He opens it, letting me through.

The guard leads me through winding hallways. "First, you must be registered," the guard says monotonously, as if he's reciting a speech. "Then, you will have a two-week intensive training camp to prepare yourself for your mission." He leads me into the front office. There is a woman sitting behind a desk.

The guard mumbles something, and she looks up. "Oh, Jeffrey!" the woman behind the desk smiles, looking at Jeffrey the guard, "what brings you here?"

"I'm escorting this young lady here. She's to be enrolled," Jeffrey takes an envelope from his pocket and hands it to her.

"Nice seeing you around," the woman behind the desk says as Jeffrey the Guard leaves. She examines the content of the envelope, and nods. "Let's get you started then," she says, grinning.

"Um, they said to give this to you," I say, handing her the shard of glass the Embassy lady gave to me earlier.

"Oh! So you're a. . ." the woman says, taking it and setting it on her desk. "Well, we have a slightly different enrollment process for you, then."

She stands up and introduces herself. She tells me to call her Carla.

"Okay," I reply as she leads me into a room next door.

"What kind of Transmorgifer are you?" she asks as she sits me down on a chair next to a complicated-looking machine.

"How . . . how did you know?" I ask.

"That shard of glass you gave me. It's universal code for people on the 'inside.' It can mean a whole bunch of things. First of all, it's a way for Transmorgifers to identify themselves. If it's sitting on a window pane outside a building, that means the building is safe," Carla says, fiddling with the machine. "Anyway, please answer the question. I assume you know what kind you are."

"Aniversi," I reply.

"Hm. I've never heard of that kind before. It's rare, I guess?" she asks.

"My brother and I are the only two alive," I say. She places my arm in a tube in the machine, kind of like a healing tube.

"See, in Lochbion, they're *nowhere* when it comes to the science of Transmorgifers," Carla explains, tapping the screen. *Tell me about it, honey.* "This little machine here confirms what kind you are for sure."

In moments, words pop up on a screen on the machine. A voice says, "Transmorgifer. Aniversi. Capability of turning into any type of animal."

"Animals? That's pretty cool," Carla says. "You can take your arm out of the tube now," she tells me.

"Now, we're going to have an assessment of your powers just to see where you stand," Carla explains. She grabs a paper that was printed from the machine which confirmed my kind, and leads me into another room.

This one is significantly larger, and unlike the other, it's almost completely empty. She leads me into the middle of the room, and goes off and stands next to the wall. "You're now going to show examples of your powers so we can place you in the proper program," Carla explains.

"What do you want me to do?" I ask her.

"Let's just warm up and start with a dog," she says, reading off the paper she has. Instinctively, I'm shrinking down, and my back is bending forward. I'm a dog. It feels nice being able to use my powers again, because I haven't had the opportunity to while I was in Camp Takes or recovery.

"Now switch to a cat," Carla reads. *Hm . . . I've never tried going directly from one animal to another. Let's try it out then.* This one takes a little bit longer, but soon enough, I'm shrinking to the ground and I'm a little kitten.

"I did it!" I say, but it comes out as a cute little "meow!"

"Okay, turn back into a human," she says. In moments, I'm plain old Sophia again.

"Let's try a bit harder one now. Elephant," Carla smiles.

Challenge accepted. Good thing this room is large. It takes only a moment of concentration before Carla starts shrinking and shrinking, and I'm getting bigger and bigger. As I change form, I don't even need to close my eyes anymore. It feels so natural, like I was born to do this. (Hereditarily speaking, I was.)

The shrinking stops, and my back is bent over. I'm actually a bit scared because I'm so tall, and the ground is so far away. "AWESOME!" Carla calls up.

And then I'm shrinking. "How are you feeling?" she says as I return to normal. "We don't want you going Haywire."

"A little bit tired, but I think I'm fine," I say, my knees shaking a bit.

"Oh! That reminds me. Can you Brainwash?" Carla asks.

I snicker for a moment, and I say, "I'm the worst at Brainwashing."

"You, know, you could just be brainwashing me while saying that," Carla says. This makes me laugh, a strange sensation I haven't felt in a very long time.

"But seriously, I'm okay at it, but not the best. My brother Shawn is who's really good at it. He'll be arriving soon, "I say. *And hopefully with Emma.*

"That's great," Carla says. "We just have one last orientation test you have to go through." She leads me into a different room. This one has a machine like the one in the first room, but this one's much bigger. Instead of an arm, this one looks like it could fit a whole human.

"I'm going to assume I have to step into the machine?" I ask.

"You assume correctly," Carla says as she steps over to a screen and starts programming the machine to do something.

As I step in, Carla begins to explain. "This one assesses your physical strength. It'll only take a moment," she says.

Darn, why couldn't they have had this kind of technology at Camp Takes? I wonder as she finishes setting it up.

There's a quick flash of light as it scans my body. Carla has results instantly. "Let's see. you're normally not an athletic person, but your powers have increased your senses and athletic abilities, correct?" she asks me.

"Right on," I say. She motions me out of the machine, and leads me out of the room again. I notice that there's a red star that's been inked onto the back of my hand, and I ask her about it.

"That indicates what program you'll be placed in to get the most out of your two weeks here," Carla explains. We're now at the end of the hallway. "I'm afraid this is where we must say goodbye. Another one of the permanent initiates is here to give you a tour of the Hall." Carla leads me through one final door, and there's a girl sitting on a bench next to it.

"Thank you, Lucy," Carla says, and she gives me off to the girl. Carla quickly strides back to the door and back to her front office.

"Hi," the girl says. She stands up and smiles, "I'm Lucy Ivandale," she says.

"As in . . ." I say, remembering the name of the place.

"Yes, as in Ivandale Hall," she says. "My dad owns this place."

"Oh," I say.

Lucy has shoulder-length straight brown hair with side-swept bangs. She has a nice, genuine smile on her face, and the way she smiles tells me she laughs a lot. She looks to be only twelve, but she could be younger. She's wearing a black shirt, black cargo pants, and black boots.

"I'm Sophia," I say.

"Well, let's give you a tour," she says. "You were just in the Orientation Hall, where they run a few tests to determine what program to put you in." She takes my right hand and looks at the red star on it.

"Good, you're in the same program as I am," she says, holding up the small red star on her hand. "There are four kinds of programs. There's the two-star program, which is for people who need lots of help with their training and acquiring new skills. There's also the one-star program, which is for initiates who need not as much help, but are here to advance the skills they already have. If your star or stars are red, it means you're a Transmorgifer. Blue ones are just normal humans."

"Well, thanks for explaining that," I say.

"We're in the main Hall right now," Lucy says, gesturing the huge hallway we're in right now. She starts walking down the hall, beckoning for me to come along.

As we walk, she explains more. "To our left is the dining Hall," she says, pointing to a door. Because all of the doors look alike, I know I'm going to have fun making my way around here.

"There are seven different training Halls. Three of them are down here, and four on the next level. You're going to be only on the upper floor," she explains.

We stop in front of a door that obviously is an elevator. She presses the button, and immediately, the doors open, letting us in.

"Actually, the top and bottom floors are almost identical, but the upper floor is where the Transmorgifers train. But the normal humans don't know that, though," Lucy says as we shoot up to the top floor.

As the door opens, Lucy asks, "What kind of Transmorgifer are you?"

"Aniversi," I reply.

"Isn't that one really rare?" she asks.

"Yeah. My brother and I are the only ones alive," I say.

"Wow, that's a pretty rare form, right? I'm just a Biomorph," Lucy explains. She leads me down the upper floor's main Hall. "To our right is the physical training Hall. Basically, this is where they bulk you up."

"Physical training?" I whisper, as images of terrible memories of Coach Gime race through my head.

"Next is the agility training Hall. This is where they train your agility, balance, and hand-eye coordination," Lucy says, pointing to another door.

"This third Hall is where they train you in firearms and weaponry," Lucy says, as we continue down the main Hall.

"And last, but not least, the Transmorgifer's Hall. This is where they help you specifically with your powers. This one is my favorite. Obviously, there's not one downstairs, because they're not Transmorgifers," she explains, pointing to the final door in the upper main Hall.

"I guess I should show you to your dorm," Lucy says. There's *another* door at the end of the hallway that she leads me through.

"This is a lot of doors to keep track of," I say, as she leads me through *another* hallway. This time, the doors have numbers on them.

"Each initiate gets their own rooms. They told me you had room 99," she says, as we stop at a door with the number 99 engraved on it.

Inside is a nice-sized room, about four times bigger than my old dorm at school. There's a bathroom to my right, and a lounge space with a few couches, and a large bed at the end of the room, and a window at the very far end of the room.

"Wow," I say. "This is great."

"Yeah, it's nice, isn't it?" Lucy says. "Dinner will be ready at seven. You'd better change into initiate uniform, otherwise you might get into trouble. If you get lost, follow all the other initiates, and you'll be fine. There's only about 100 of us. I hope to see you there."

Lucy then exits the room. "That was a lot of Halls, doors, and rooms," I mumble to myself.

This place seems a lot like my old school, but I know this place will be so much better.

Chapter 17

~

Lucy

Lucy's heart is pounding and her palms are sweating. Hopefully, her father won't be able to tell. She has just dropped off Sophia, and she's going to talk to him. Lucy is determined to get some truth out of him. She's determined to know what he really thinks of her.

And it'll be easy, because Mr. Ivandale won't be talking to Lucy because she doesn't look like Lucy. She's Transmorgified into Commander Joy, the head of the red one-star initiates.

She steps into her father's office; it's a cold and solemn place. He sits there at a desk, working, and doesn't bother to look at her.

"Excuse me, Mr. Ivandale," Lucy says. She discreetly bites her lip because she sounds like a 40-year old man.

"Yes?" her father looks up from his work.

"I'd like to report something," Lucy says, disguised as Commander Joy. "Your daughter, Lucy. She's been goofing off in class again."

"Argh," Her father says. "Don't remind me. That child is too insensible. She'll never be able to succeed like I want her to."

Lucy's using all the self-control she can muster not to yell at her father. "Yes, sir," she replies in the ultra-manly voice she's newly acquired. "I just thought you might want to know." She exits the office. She runs back to her dorm, with a number 85 on it, and shuts it. She turns back into herself.

Okay, maybe she does goof off a bit in class, but not that much. Maybe she does talk about books she has read and makes jokes and sings songs, but she's still getting her training done.

But is that really what her father thinks about her?

~

Sophia

I figure that I have to change into the clothes Lucy mentioned. I walk over to a closet, and open it up. There's an outfit exactly like the one Lucy was wearing, so I change into it. There's a polyester black shirt that has sleeves that go down to the top of my elbows. On the back is a single medium-sized red star in the center. Above that is the word, "LORAIN" in red lettering. There's also black cargo pants with too many pockets to count. Along with this is a pair of cozy black socks and combat boots.

After changing, I take a look at the time. It's 6:19. So I sit and wait around for a half an hour before going down. Lucy said that dinner is at 7. I exit the room, and look down the hall.

There's some other people heading back to the upper floor of the main Hall. I still don't really know where everything is, so I decide to follow them.

"Sophia!" I hear a voice call out as I follow people through the doors of the dining Hall. Hopefully it's Shawn or Emma, but when I turn around, it's Lucy.

"Hi, Lucy," I say.

"Come on, let's get dinner," she says. "I'm starving."

As I enter the dining room, I immediately like the feel of this one better than the one at my old school. There are circular tables instead of rectangular ones, so everybody can have a say in the conversation. It seems like all the initiates get along nicely, and I immediately notice that I'm one of the youngest here. It seems like the people here are older, probably 17 or 18 years old. Still, with the few amount of younger people, they all seem to be friends.

Tonight there is a thick and creamy chicken and rice soup, served up in large bowls with bits of cheese scattered on top. Along with that, we get a fresh, steamy roll.

After following Lucy through the line and getting the soup and rolls, I walk behind her as she goes to a table.

And sitting at this particular table are Shawn and Emma. "Shawn! Emma!" I say, as I sit down next to them. They're dressed initiate clothing, just as I am. A sigh of relief runs through me. They must have agreed to do the mission anyways.

"Hey, Sophia," Shawn says as he hugs me. Lucy sits down next to me.

"Shawn, Emma, this is Lucy," I say, gesturing to my right.

"Hi," Shawn and Emma say.

"Hi," says Lucy.

Other people start to sit down at the table with us. They're all older than us, but they seem to be good friends with Lucy, and she kind of brings us into the group.

As we all eat our soup and rolls, I have a chance of meeting the other initiates. They all seem friendly enough, although I can't remember half of their names.

Shawn, being Shawn, warms up to them almost instantly. He's back being the old Shawn: cool and popular. It's nice to see his face light up as we have all sorts of conversations.

Emma seems to be enjoying herself. I have to remind myself to ask Shawn what convinced her.

"What program are you three in?" one of the older guys asks. I think his name is Jared.

"Uh, red star," I say. Apparently Shawn and Emma are in the same as me.

"Cool, I'm in the blue star," Jared says. *So he must be a normal human, then.*

As I look around the room and look at the back of people's shirts, I see that there are more people with blue stars than red. I guess there's about twice as much humans than

ANIVERSI

Transmorgifers, which makes sense, considering that being a Transmorgifer is really rare.

I also realize this must be the largest gathering of Transmorgifers ever. Since we left, there's only eight or nine campers at Camp Takes, and I can see there's definitely more than that here.

After dinner, Lucy gives Shawn and Emma a tour. They only had enough time to get here, get orientated, and change before going to dinner. "Stop by my room any time you like!" Lucy tells me before she begins the tour. "I'm room 85." I decide to head back to my room.

It's nice having a room all to myself. Better than having to share one a fourth of the size with four times as many people.

Right next to the door where I enter is a monitor. I notice it because it bleeps when I come in, showing a message on it. I bend down and look at what it says. "DAILY SCHEDULE. TAP TO RECEIVE."

I tap the screen, and a small slip of paper prints out from the bottom of the machine. On the sheet of paper has the daily schedule I will use for the next two weeks of my training here.

As I read through it, I have a huge sigh of relief. I get to sleep in a whole extra hour than I did at the school in Lochbion. I'm disappointed when I find out I get an hour and a half of physical training, like I did back in Lochbion. I figure it must be better than my old school since everything here is better.

Ivandale Hall Schedule

SOPHIA LORAIN

6:30 AM: All initiates rise. Inspection.

6:50 AM: Breakfast

7:30 AM: Knives in Weaponry Hall

8:00 AM: Firearms in Weaponry Hall

9:00 AM: Hand-Eye coordination in Agility Hall

10:00 AM: Balance in Agility Hall

10:30 AM: Physical Training Hall

12:00 PM: Lunch/Break

1:00 PM: Special training in Transmorgifer's Hall

2:30 PM: Free-For-All session

4:00 PM: Specialty Training

5:00 PM: Extra Help Training

6:00 PM: Down time in dorm rooms

7:00 PM: Dinner

8:00 PM: Down time in rec-room

9:00 PM: All must return to dorms

    There are some things I'm not sure of what they are, such as the Free-For-All session, but I figure I'll catch onto things quickly enough.

    After scrolling through my schedule, I find that there's a shower in the bathroom adjacent to my room. I take a few minutes to rinse off and clean myself, and afterwards, I find that there are pajamas provided for me in the closet I found the initiate uniform in. It's a basic long-sleeved shirt and black sweatpants, but it's actually comfortable and fits quite well. *I wonder how they knew what size I was*. I think as I crawl into the large, comfortable bed.

The time's only 8:36, but I'm completely exhausted from the day. It seems strange that only this morning they released me out of rehab at the Healing Center in the smack center of Sector Six. The day's been entirely too long and there are certain parts of it I'd rather not remember, but it's only moments before I drift off into a deep sleep.

~

You know that feeling you get when you wake up in the middle of the night and you realize you still have an hour left of sleep?

I'm just experiencing that feeling right now. It's 5:25 AM, and since my body is programmed to wake up then, I obviously do. Even though I've never had to wake up that early in a while, it still does that. Maybe it's just that I'm a morning person.

After I'm up, I can't fall back asleep. Perhaps that also has something to do with this 5:25 in the morning thing engraved into my brain. I kind of lay in my bed, cozy under the warm covers for a while.

I remember back to that awful day when my school tried to kill me, how that morning I wished more than anything to have twenty minutes of extra sleep. It's funny that now I have the opportunity for an hour of extra sleep, but I can't even fall asleep.

I stand up and get out of bed for a moment, only to go over to a table where I left my daily schedule. I take the rest of the time I have before there's inspection to memorize it. I have a feeling that's going to be convenient. I hardly know the place, and not knowing what I have and when I have it is only going to make that situation worse.

There is a loud and long BUZZ! coming from an intercom. I'm guessing this is supposed to be my signal to wake up. I check the clock, and sure enough, it's 6:30. Quickly, I get up from my bed and walk out to the outside of my room.

I see that the room across from mine, room 100, is where Emma is slouching. She's got her strawberry blonde hair all over her face and dark circles under her eyes. I know that she's most definitely not a morning person and loves sleeping, so this transition of waking up early must be difficult.

"Emma," I say. "I didn't know you were across from me."

"Me neither," she says, rubbing her eyes.

Memories flash back from when I had to have inspection everyday back at school. It feels a bit odd at first, but when I don't hear the screaming voices of the hallway inspectors like Mrs. Moraine, I'm assured.

"Are all of you out here?" a calm voice calls from down the hall. The chattering there was dies down, just as it did every morning at my old school in Lochbion.

"Say 'I' if you're still in your room and asleep," the woman says.

Instinctively, almost every voice, including mine, chimes back, "I!" There's a little bit of laughter and giggles.

"Remember, guys, breakfast is at 6:50, not 6:53. Please don't dawdle," the inspector calls. "Go ahead and get ready."

I take a moment and stop to talk with Emma. "How are you doing?" I ask.

"Fine, I guess. I'm still not sure I want to go on this mission thing," she says.

"Maybe training here will change your mind," I say.

"Or maybe it won't," she retorts.

"I think we have to get ready. I'll see you at breakfast," I tell her. I quickly run back into my room to avoid any more tense conversations with Emma. I go ahead and get ready. There's a toothbrush and toothpaste and all those little goodies in the bathroom, so I brush my teeth and comb my hair before changing. There's a new initiate uniform in the closet. I quickly slap it on and decide to go to Lucy's room before I head to breakfast.

I knock on the door that has 85 on it. "Come on in," says Lucy. I open the door, and she's sitting on a couch in her room.

"I had a feeling you'd come before breakfast. Still a bit lost getting there?" she asks.

"Yeah," I admit.

"That's all right," she says. "Come on, let's get going." It looks like Lucy's already dressed and ready to go, so we head down to the dining Hall.

"Be warned: breakfasts here are porridge. Lunch and dinner are awesome, but breakfast is simply porridge. Every day. My dad thinks it's good for you or whatever, but I think it's disgusting," Lucy explains to me, making a bit of a face. *That's right. Her dad owns this place.*

"I have a question. Why is it that there's practically 17 and 18 year olds besides you, Shawn, Emma, and I?" I ask her.

"Well, we typically don't enroll initiates as young as us. They're still in school, you know. My dad plucked me out of school when I was eleven and stuck me in here. Normally, you train here for two years, but I'm going to be here for six instead. I guess I'm going to be an agent for Terranary when I get older," she explains.

"To even get into this school is really difficult. The government has to specifically seek you out, and see if you show the talent and if you want to do it. Even after two years of training here, some people still don't make it onto the international police force, which is where most people are aiming. I guess you and your brother and your friend are lucky," she explains some more as we go through the line in the dining room.

Lucy was right: breakfast food here is boring. They give us bowls of gray oatmeal, and to be honest, it's pretty disgusting. But after my experience at Camp Takes, I never refuse any food. Ever.

"They divide us up by program and gender. Since we're both girls in the Red Star program, we're going to have the same schedule," Lucy says as we exit the dining hall.

"Good. That means we're also with Emma," I tell her. We head back upstairs for our first lesson.

Weaponry Hall is huge. It has the largest assortment of weapons I've seen in my life, even larger than the weapon room back at school. There are all kinds of guns you could imagine: from simple stun-guns to a machine gun.

There's four other older girls besides Lucy, Emma, and I with a red star on the back of their shirt, or inked onto the back of their hand. We all circle around a station in the room with "Knives" on a sign above it.

Honestly, this station is kind of terrifying. There are knives of all size, some small, and some large. They're made of all kinds of metal, and they look extremely dangerous.

In this class, we're trained to properly throw knives, wield them, and conceal them. The instructor tells me that I will be terrible at first, but once I practice more in agility Hall, I will get better. He assigns me homework: spend most of my time in agility working on my aim.

And he's certainly right. When I first try throwing a knife, I almost hit somebody. The instructor has me learn how to wield a knife, and save throwing them for later.

This first class is over before I know it, and to be quite honest, it was enjoyable. I move over to the other side of weaponry Hall, along with the other six girls in my program.

In Year G, they begin teaching you basics of gunmanship, so I have rudimentary knowledge of what everybody's doing. I catch onto what they're doing easily enough. On the mission, however, I'm going to be given a stun-gun, and not a real gun. The instructor has me spend half the time with real guns, and half the time with a stun-gun.

The rest of the morning consists of training in agility Hall, and training in the physical training Hall. In agility Hall, they have a bunch of balance exercises and they have us pitch balls and do other tests for hand-eye coordination. I do what the knife instructor told me to do, and I spend a whole forty-five minutes pitching softballs.

At first, my aim is terrible, but one of the agility instructors helps me with my pitch, and it becomes a lot better. By the end of my pitching session, I have a pretty good aim, and I'm ready to start actually throwing knives tomorrow.

The physical training Hall is not as bad as I thought it was going to be. They don't force you to play any sports. Actually, you're not playing sports at all. You're doing exercises to bulk up on high-tech machines, running around the track surrounding the room, and there's even a 25 yard long pool where you can do laps in there. We're allowed to do what we want, but we have to get in half our time doing cardio and the other half muscle-building.

The only downside of physical training Hall is the instructor, who forces people to address him as Commander Joy. In short, this man is most certainly not joyful. Lucy, Emma and I go off and do our own thing, trying to avoid him as much as possible.

Although this Hall is my least favorite, it's not as bad as Physical Training at my old school, where I'd be stuck failing at sports for an hour and a half each day. With my newly acquired Transmorgifer powers, my senses have sharpened and my physical strength and endurance have increased exponentially. Although I'm still not some star athlete, I'm not as mediocre as I used to be.

After physical training hall is lunch. Good. I'm starving. Lucy's right about meals here: Lunch and dinner are great, but breakfast is pitiful. I can feel that Shawn, Emma, and I are beginning to feel accepted within the initiates. They're kind of like a large army of big siblings, but unfortunately, they're only going to be that for the next two weeks.

~~

Chapter 18

~

Emma

As Emma goes through her first day at Ivandale Hall, she quickly gets accustomed to everything, except for maybe the part about waking up early every morning.

Every time that she is haunted by memories and doesn't want to go back to Lochbion, she remembers the conversation, if you could call it that, that she and Shawn had earlier this morning:

The time was 3:47 AM. She was breaking the rules on one of her day here, and Emma knew it. She snuck out of her room. But she promised to meet with Shawn. Emma never gets to see him, except for at meals and downtime, which is to say, never. The rules here at Ivandale clearly state if a girl is going into a boy's room, they can't be alone, other people must in there, and the door has to be open.

Shawn's room is number 49. As she stood outside his room, she quietly gave a small knock. The door immediately opened, and Shawn was standing there, with frazzled hair and a tired look on his face, but Emma didn't care. He looked gorgeous anyway. She rushed in and Shawn shut the door.

"Emma," he said, hugging her.

"I still don't want to go on this mission they want us to do," she said, letting go of his embrace and looking at him. "I can't stand going back into that awful country."

Shawn stared down into her green eyes and smiled. "We'll be fine," he said. "Lochbion has a crap load of security, but we know what the building is like, and Terranary has the technology to crack it."

She didn't say anything. Silence is acceptance.

"Emma," he said, "we're going to be just fine. You'll see."

She stared up into his gorgeous blue eyes. When he bent down and pressed his lips against hers, she knew that everything might be all right.

At least, right then, at that moment, it was.

~

Sophia

After lunch and a quick break, Lucy escorts Emma and I to what is soon to be my favorite training Hall: the Transmorgifer's Hall. Scattered around the room different stations, one for each kind of Transmorgifer. There is a section for Biomorphs, Chlorophists, and other forms that I've never heard of such as Medimorphs and Abiomorphs. Finally, I find the one entitled, "Aniversi." That station is empty.

As I stand there, waiting for class to begin, one of the trainers comes up to me. "You're that newbie who's the Aniversi, right?" he asks.

"Yeah."

"Wow. Two new Aniversi in one day," he says.

"Well," I explain, "the other one you're talking about must be my brother."

"Shawn?" he asks. "I could tell. You two look like siblings."

While we being the training session, I find most of the initiates training with me are Biomorphs, with Chlorophists coming in a close second. There are two mediomorphs; people who can partially change into certain forms. There aren't any Abiomorphs, but I learn that kind is able to change into non-living things.

Training in the Transmorgifer Hall consists of half an hour of various exercises to help amp up your speed and accuracy when it comes to Transmorgifying, as well as quickly adapting to the thing you're changing into. Emma spends half her time with the Biomorphs, and spends the other half of her time with me.

"Emma, why didn't you tell me you had Aniversi powers?" I ask her. I've talked with her after the plane crash, and I've found that in addition to having Aniversi powers, Emma gained the ability to Brainwash, which she didn't have before. In addition, the strange gases and drugs that are supposed to prevent Transmorgifying at Camp Takes don't work on her anymore. They must've seriously messed up the first procedure they did on her for that to happen.

"I wanted to forget my first experience at Camp Takes," she explains. "I was extremely surprised when I found out I had extra powers after an operation went wrong. I had such terrible experiences there, I pretended like I didn't have those powers. I only used them when I absolutely had to."

Emma doesn't talk to me for the rest of the session.

After this, there's a half an hour cool down so we don't go Haywire. It's basically thirty minutes of doing nothing. I guess you can talk to other initiates , but they kind of want us to sit down and rest so we don't die. Then, it's simply another half an hour of training again. The third half hour, the Transmorgifers who can Brainwash (Which is only three others besides Emma and me) also have the opportunity of training with that. I utilize that time well, because I'm not that good at Brainwashing.

After training in Transmorgifer's Hall, there is a Free-For-All session. We can do whatever we like in any of the Halls except for Transmorgifer's, because they don't want us going Haywire or get over-exhausted. Emma meets up with Shawn in weaponry Hall, and I decide to go to agility Hall with Lucy. Free-For-All is an hour and a half, and I spend most of that time just pitching balls with Lucy so I can work on hand-eye coordination. Maybe the next time I try throwing knives, I'll have more precise aim..

By the end of Free-For-All, I'm pretty exhausted from the day, but I still have two sessions remaining: Specialty and Extra-Help. Specialty is basically where they determine where your strengths lie, and they give you extra training to help you with that. I guess they found me better than I thought I did at Brainwashing, so they call me back to Transmorgifer's Hall so I can get better at that.

Then comes Extra-Help. You guessed it, they ship me straight off to the Physical Training hall to bulk me up some more. I spend this time doing laps in the pool, because I can go slow and warm down from the long day.

Afterwards, I'm about to drop down dead because I'm so exhausted. I slump back to my dorm for a while to rest before dinner. I guess that being at Ivandale Hall is tiring. There's lots of training that must be done for Shawn, Emma, and I to be whipped into shape for the secret agent mission Terranary is having us do.

Probably the main difference between my school in Lochbion and Ivandale Hall is that nobody hates me at Ivandale Hall. It's a strange and new feeling. And I think that I like it.

But after dinner, initiates are allowed to go to the rec-room for a while if they'd like, but I'm so exhausted I head straight back up to my room. I put on the new pair of pajamas that have appeared in my closet, and head straight back to bed.

ANIVERSI

As I lie in my bed, I think about how nice it is to actually fall asleep by myself, and not have some strange drug coursing through my body forcing me to sleep.

~

I become accustomed to life at Ivandale Hall very quickly. Soon enough, I don't have to follow Lucy around everywhere because I know where everything is. The days become relatively normal, and I can manage by myself.

I also happen to make lots of new friends. Although they're all older than me, they're nice and treat me like a little sister. They're also very awesome at the games in the rec-room, so I usually hang out with them after dinner most nights.

But there is one night where instead of going to hang out in the rec-room, Shawn approaches me instead as soon as I enter.

"Can I speak with you?" he asks, and drags me out of the room. We go down the hallway and towards the boy's dorm hall.

It's a policy that we have to keep our doors open if we're going into somebody else's room. It's also policy that we have to have other people in the room with us. It's a good thing that Shawn decides to stop when we reach the end of the main hall so we can talk there, and not in one of our rooms. It makes me a bit nervous, because somebody could overhear us, and from the looks on Shawn's face, the conversation he wants to have is definitely not something that he wants to be overheard.

"There's something I'd like to talk with you about," Shawn says.

"Yes?" I ask.

"Well, let's just say, Emma's not so happy you've dragged us into this mission," Shawn says. "I've talked with her, and I've tried to reason with her, but she won't budge." That's surprising. I thought that Emma was okay with going on this mission, since there's almost no way it could fail.

"Well, what can we do about it now?" I ask. "Tell them to call it off?"

"No, I wasn't suggesting that. Honestly, I don't really want to go on this mission either," Shawn says.

"So it'll just be me," I say. "Fine."

"No, I'm not asking for that!" Shawn says. He slides down the wall we're standing next to and sits down.

"The main reason I called you out here is to ask you something. What was going through your head when you pushed Emma and I into doing this mission?" Shawn asks me.

"You know, I guess it's that I want to help people. I remember how hopeless I was in Camp Takes, and I figured I could save a few lives. Honestly, if Emma wasn't some special form of Transmorgifer whose powers still work in Camp Takes, I'd be the one who needs to be saved!" I tell Shawn.

"I guess I just don't want you to get hurt," he says.

"And I don't want you to get hurt either," I say. "We can't just call it off, though. I've talked with Lucy, and she says we're very lucky to be in Ivandale at this age. It's extremely difficult to get in here, even if you're 17 or 18. I guess that in the end, we can strengthen up our powers or something," I say.

"I guess so," Shawn says.

"Just please, talk with Emma," I say. "You're the one who can convince her."

"I'll talk with her," he tells me. "I might not be able to convince her, though."

"Yes you will," I say. "Trust me. I've seen the way you two talk to each other. She just lights up whenever she's around you." Shawn's cheeks turn a bit pink.

"I thought you didn't know."

"Are you kidding? Of course I know what's going on with you two," I say.

"Fine, fine! I'll talk to her! Stop pressuring me!"

~~

Chapter 19

~

Lucy

"Dad?" Lucy calls, knocking on the thick wooden door to her father's office.

"Yes?" her father replies. "Come on in." She quickly shoves open the door and strides over to her father's desk.

"You remember our agreement?" Lucy asks, tapping her fingers nervously on her father's desk. "If I worked especially hard these past two weeks, then you'd let me go on that mission with Sophia, Shawn, and Emma."

"Yes, I recall that," Lucy's dad says, not looking up from his computer screen. "I've gotten reports from your trainers. It seems that you've been behaving and not goofing off as much."

"I'm not goofing off, dad!" Lucy protests. "I'm just trying to make training more interesting. Life gets a bit monotonous having the same schedule six days a week for the past two years."

Lucy's father looks up from his computer, and glares into Lucy's eyes. *Oh great, now I've done it,* she thinks. *There's no way I'm going on this mission.*

"You'd better hurry up then," he says, with a trickle of a smile on his face. "I think the trio already left a few minutes ago. You can ask another driver to get you back into Prudence. Best you go on then."

Lucy's heart jumps with glee. *I can go on the mission,* she thinks. *I can actually do something besides train!*

~

Today was my last day at Ivandale Hall. My schedule was completely normal, except directly after dinner, they ship Shawn, Emma, and I off to Prudence to prepare for our mission. We have to meet with the Embassy before we go on our mission.

Honestly, I'm a little bit scared. Even though we have a general idea of what the interior of Camp Takes is like, I hear the security is still top-notch. I know that if I ever become a camper there again, the first thing they'll do is slice me up again and then stick me back in that starvation chamber so they can finish off what they started.

As Shawn, Emma, and I get into the back-seat of the car, the windows blacken up as they did before.

"So this is it," I say, looking at Shawn and Emma. Shawn looks pretty confident, but Emma still looks a bit tense. She's squeezing Shawn's hand tightly.

I stare at the window. I can't look out it since it's been blackened out, but I need to do something. It feels extremely awkward with Shawn and Emma being glued together, and I'm sitting inches from them. Part of me wants to stare at them with disgust, and the other part of me wants to break down and cry. I can hear them whispering as the car begins to move.

You're being stupid. Why should you cry? I mentally beat myself, trying to figure out why I'm feeling these pathetic feelings. I take a peek looking at them, but this only makes me feel more lonely. *Now you're being really stupid. Shawn, Emma, and Lucy are all your friends. How can you feel so lonely?*

As we sit there in silence, whirlwinds of thoughts and feelings churn through me. Finally, I tell myself to calm down. I force my eyes shut, and I lean my head against the freezing window. I take a moment to appreciate the silence and stop thinking stupid thoughts. The past few months have been too hectic. There's noise all of the time. It's nice to have some time in total silence.

~

After a while, Shawn decides to break the stillness. "I'm going to miss Lucy. She was nice," he says.

"She was," I say. "It'd be awesome if she could come with us. She's had so much experience and training."

But nothing else is said until we arrive. We're let out of the car and back into the Embassy's building. The three of us are back in Prudence.

ANIVERSI

I notice the shard of glass sitting next to the window as I enter. It's supposed to guarantee safety for Transmorgifers, but I'm about to test that promise and be departed on an extremely dangerous mission. We're lead back into the Embassy meeting room: number 119. Commander Carvenaw and other members are already seated in there. Shawn, Emma, and I take three of the open seats, the ones at the foot of the table in the front of the room.

"Welcome," Commander Carvenaw says. "Today is the day we deport you back to Lochbion to save the campers from Camp Takes. Are you three ready?"

"Yes," all three of us say, somewhat hesitant.

"Good," says Carvenaw, oblivious to our doubtfulness. "We're going to begin with our plan of attack." A blue-tinted holograph appears out of nowhere, showing a 360 degree three-dimensional figure of Camp Takes..

"You three have to know that we've been working on this project for years. We couldn't execute it until now because we weren't sure about some of the security issues with Lochbion, we didn't have anybody right for the job, and none of us have actually been to Camp Takes," one of the women sitting around the table explains.

"We have recently created a small aircraft specially designed to defeat Lochbion's Air Force security system." A holograph of the aircraft appears. "It can travel at immense speeds, hold fifteen passengers comfortably, and can even turn invisible. We'll drop you three onto the roof-"

"WAIT!" somebody yells, barging the door open.

It's Lucy.

"I'm coming too," she says. "My father just gave permission."

"Yes, I got that message. I was about to tell you three," Carvenaw says, pointing to us. "Lucy, why don't you come and sit down? We're explaining our plan of attack at the moment."

Lucy sits down next to me. *Lucy's coming* I think. *This mission is going to be so much more easy!*

"There are three things that must be accomplished. First: the Transmorgifers must be rescued. This is the most important thing. Half of you will venture out to where they are. At the current time, there aren't any tests running. Three of them are in starvation chambers due to being disobedient. Six of them are in recovery from being tested on, and one is being prepped to start operations. Direct locations of the campers will be told Shawn and Emma, who will help rescue them," Carvenaw tells us. The holographic 3D diagram of Camp Takes has ten different places being highlighted, probably where the Transmorgifers are.

"The second thing that must get done is deletion of the files that the doctors have acquired over the years. If all their files are deleted, it will be extremely difficult to start again," he tells us. "The main file room is located here, but again, more details will be given later to Lucy and Sophia, who will be in charge of this aspect." The ten spots that were previously lit up disappear, and another lights up, showing where the files are stored.

"I just have a real quick question," Shawn asks, staring at the hologram.

"Yes?"

"Lochbion is going to think this is some sort of terrorist attack, right? What are we going to do about that?"

"Don't worry. We've got that completely covered," Carvenaw says, smiling. "Brainwashing. We'll give them a taste of their own medicine."

~

After the meeting, I'm beginning to feel very confident in what needs to happen. Lucy, Emma, Shawn and I are dismissed to go get suited up. Apparently they have these awesome high-tech agent suits we're to wear, with wireless transmitters so we can speak with the people back at home-base, and complete with a stun-gun (because fourteen year olds are *obviously* too young to be handling real guns) and a couple of throwing knives. It's the epitome of an awesome agent suit.

Emma, Lucy, and I are led into one room, while Shawn into another. They seem to know my size, like they did at

Ivandale, because the suit I'm to wear fits perfectly when I slide it on. It's skin-tight, and extremely comfortable. There's also a headset somebody attaches around my ears with a communicator, with these glasses that make it a little bit easier to see in the dark, and a tiny screen where I can see what's behind me.

So after we're suited up, we're loaded onto the small aircraft the commander was talking about earlier. There are fifteen seats crammed into the back, and two pilots up-front.

"Are you ready?" the pilot asks.

"Yes," we all call back.

So then the pilot takes off. We're leaving Terranary.

And going back into Lochbion.

Chapter 20

~

Pilots

"I don't think these kids know what they're getting themselves into," says the pilot to his co-pilot.

"Well, we got into Lochbion okay," the co-pilot observes. "Maybe they do know what they're getting into."

"Oh, come on. Don't fool yourself. Camp Takes is a madhouse with crazy good security. Even if they get in, there's no way they're getting out."

"Three of them have gotten out before, and one of those three has been in twice. I think they know what they're doing," the co-pilot asserts. "Maybe the security isn't as tight as you think it is. Back in Prudence, they're already doing all they can to disable security and make this go as smooth as possible."

"Whatever you think," the pilot remarks. "But if we die, I'm gonna kill you."

~

Sophia

The ride back into Lochbion is quick, tense, and silent. My heart is pounding and racing as we silently and quickly fly through the air. Shawn, Emma, Lucy and I are the only ones sitting in the passenger seats, and the thing that assures me about this mission is by the end of it, there will be thirteen sitting back here instead of four.

I notice how anxious Emma is, because the last time we flew somewhere, Jessaline and Gracie died. I force myself to be strong, because I know this must be hard for her.

It seems like only minutes before the pilot speaks to us over the sound system. "We'll be arriving in a few moments. We have been undetected by Lochbion's security systems so far, which is a good thing. I guess they're just being lazy tonight. Prepare yourselves for the drop."

They told us about 'the drop' back in Terranary. We had to go to the side door of the helicopter, have the rope ladder drop from the copter, and then climb down onto the roof.

"Try to be as quick as you can in there. Don't dawdle. That way we can ditch this popsicle stand like we were never here," the co-pilot says.

The helicopter stops moving, although it is still in air.

"All right. Go ahead with the drop," the pilot orders. The side door slides open, and a gush of wind rushes into my face. Shawn takes a long rope ladder and drops it down until it reaches the roof of the building.

"I'll go first," Shawn says over the sound of the wind. Fearlessly, he exits the helicopter and drops down the ladder.

"Who's next?" Emma asks.

"I will," Lucy says, and she quickly follows after Shawn. Now it's only Emma and I in the helicopter.

"Hurry up," we can barely hear from the pilot over the sound of rushing breeze.

"I'll go," I say. Before Emma can even say anything, I'm outside the helicopter and onto the ladder. I'm extremely surprised when I remember that the helicopter is invisible, but I zoom down the ladder anyway.

My heart starts racing again as my feet touch down onto the cool rooftop. Emma's right behind me, so as soon as the four of us are on the roof, the ladder is lifted up back into the helicopter. The door shuts, and it blends in with the cool night. You can't tell the helicopter is there. *That must be why we haven't alarmed their security yet.*

Our plan goes right into action.

"Okay, begin the Transmorgifying," there a voice coming from the transmitters we have attached to our suits.

"Okay," I reply. Emma and Lucy morph into nurses here at Camp Takes. Shawn and I Transmorgify into insects, so we can follow them undetected.

"Remember," Emma says, "as soon as we enter the building, you three won't be able to change back until we disable security. There's still that gas running through the building preventing Transmorgifying."

Emma and Lucy immediately start using their stun guns to break the security cameras here on the roof. Afterwards, they find a door that leads down into the building.

Even though the four of us are Transmorgified, our transmitters still work. The person on the other side starts giving us directions to the security room, which luckily, isn't that far away.

As we go through the blank white hallways, I feel anxious and scared. If this mission failed, I would land right back in here to begin testing again.

Luckily, as we enter the dark security room, there's only one guard on duty.

"What are you doing in here?" she asks, but Emma and Lucy stun her before she can do anything else. *The pilot's right. They are being pretty lazy with security today. We're pretty lucky.*

Shawn and I change back into ourselves as Emma and Lucy shut off the rest of security. All doors are now unlocked, the strange gas going through the building is now being sucked out, and all security cameras have been disabled and all data from them have been wiped.

"One second," Lucy says. "We need to divert their attention." She sits down at one of the security computers, fiddles around for a few minutes, and suddenly, the room starts beeping piercingly loud with a wailing alarm. "Fire alarm," she smiles. "I've programmed it so it's just a drill, but the staff will think it's the real thing."

"Good thinking," says the transmitter lady. "Looking at the layouts of Camp Takes, there's a fireproof room in the basement where the staff are supposed to go during a fire alarm. Why they're not exiting the building, I have no clue. Let's just go with it then." After this, we finish disabling security.

"Part one, check," Shawn says after unplugging the plug running the security. The entire room goes dark except for a small lamp on the ceiling.

"Okay, Sophia, you and I have to go wipe the data they've collected. Emma and Shawn need to start rescuing campers," Lucy says, as she bolts out the door.

"We'll meet you back at the helicopter in twenty minutes," I say to Emma and Shawn as I follow Lucy.

"Good thing none of the campers are in testing right now," Lucy says as we bolt towards the data room. As we run, she's changing back into a nurse. I would Transmorgify back into an insect, but I might go Haywire.

We go through the silent hallways virtually undetected because the security is disabled. We have to stun a few guards who haven't made it downstairs, though, but we end up at the data room without any major complications.

Lucy enters the data room first. From what I can tell, there are people in there despite the blaring alarm, because she takes a minute or two stunning them all.

When I enter, I see three unconscious bodies on the ground in a pile, with Lucy beside them, holding a gun and smiling.

"How did you do that undetected?" I ask her.

"Well, let's just say, two years of training at Ivandale comes in handy," she says, running over to the computers with the data.

Lucy seems to be some computer whiz, because in a few moments, she's hacked into their database and is deleting all the files. After she finishes this, We spend a few minutes unplugging cables, cutting wires, and smashing computers.

On the other side of the room is a fridge full of samples that the doctors have collected. After unplugging the fridge, we knock it over, shattering everything inside of it.

"Okay, we're almost done here," Lucy says.

"Yeah, let's go to the operating room," I tell her, running out of the room. The headset transmitter lady gives us directions to go down a floor and into the operating room.

It's good that we've disabled security because only authorized individuals can access the testing lab. The hand scanner doesn't even pop up, instead the door just opens letting us in.

The fake fire alarm we pulled was supposed to have everybody exit the building, but as we enter the operation room, we see there's somebody standing there, in the middle of the aisle.

And it's the person I least want to see right now. Standing right there is Dr. Ayers, the evil creature who tortured me and sliced me up twice.

The people in Terranary said not to kill anybody if at all possible, but before I can control myself, I take out a small throwing knife and chuck it straight at Dr. Ayers before he can even turn around.

He cries out as it slices him right in the shoulder.

"Sophia! What do you think you're doing?" I hear from over the headset.

"You don't understand," I grumble back. I step towards Ayers, who's shoulder is bleeding.

"Well," he smiles, as if he's not injured. It's good he hasn't noticed Lucy yet, because she's creeping around behind the equipment to sneak up on him. "Look who came back! My star patient. Just wait here a few minutes, we can hook you up, and begin more testing! How does that sound?"

"Go to hell!" I yell at him, as Lucy creeps behind him, and in half a second, stuns him. He falls to the ground, and strangely enough, he doesn't go unconscious. He takes the knife I sliced him with earlier and jabs it into Lucy's foot. She screams in pain, and she bends over and stuns him again.

She yanks the knife out of her foot, and hobbles over to me. "Lucy, you just sit down," I tell her. "I'll destroy the equipment."

She immediately plops down and yanks off her shoe and sock. I take a sigh of relief. It's not as bad as I thought it would be, but the injury still looks pretty painful.

"Lucy just got stabbed in the foot," I speak into the transmitter.

"Tell her to keep her foot elevated," the headset lady says. "You go destroy the equipment. You know the deal, unplug, cut, shatter, knock over. Get going."

"Keep it elevated," I tell Lucy as I go over to destroy the equipment. Like the transmitter woman said, I unplug all of the equipment. I take one of my knives and start cutting the wires. After this, I smash every screen I can find, and knock over some of the complex machinery, almost completely shattering it.

"Can you connect me to Emma's transmitter?" I speak into the communicator.

"Sure," the other side says. In a few moments, there's a BEEP, and I can hear Emma's voice.

"Shawn! Can you get the last initiate? I'm going to go find Sophia and Lucy," she says through the transmitter.

"Emma!" I call into my headset. "They've hooked me up so I can speak with you. We need you on the fourth floor in the operating room. Lucy's injured, and I'm not exactly sure how to move her."

"Great. Shawn's getting the ninth camper out of here. We're not sure where the tenth one is. They must've escaped after we disabled security. I'll be right up there," she says.

It takes a few moments, but as Emma comes up, her face is grim. "The building's on fire," she says anxiously.

"What?" I yell. "How are we going to get Lucy out of here?"

"Don't worry, Sophia, I can still walk," Lucy says, trying to stand up, but her face tightens with pain and she slumps back down.

"Don't be kidding yourself. You can't walk," I say.

"The worst part of the fire?" Emma tells me, "I think the tenth camper might've started it. I'm going to go find them. Sophia, I think you can get Lucy downstairs by yourself. How does that sound?"

"I'll try," I tell her. Emma runs off, trying to find the escaped camper who possibly started the fire.

"I'm sorry if I'm hurting you," I tell Lucy as I help her up. She puts an arm around my shoulder, and slowly, we hobble along out of the building and down the hallway.

Emma's right: the building is on fire. There's smoke spreading everywhere, but I have to get Lucy onto the first floor. We head to the side of the hallway, and luckily, there's a stairwell there. It's much easier bringing her down the stairs than across a hallway. The whole time, Lucy's sweating and breathing quickly. She's very tense, and I can tell she's in a lot of pain.

Suddenly, I slip on one of the stairs, and the both of us come crashing down. Lucy screams out in pain, her face bright red with pain and tears brimming at her eyes. I try to help her up, but the first thing I notice is my ankle starts throbbing, and it doesn't feel right. It's not broken, but it could be sprained. I suck it up anyway, and help Lucy down one more flight of stairs.

By the time we get to the first floor, my ankle is agonizingly painful, but I don't care. I help Lucy outside, and I help her find the rope that the helicopter has let down. She makes her way over to the rope and climbs back into the aircraft. I'm about to join her, when I get a message from the transmitter.

"Where is Shawn?"

"You mean he's not up there in the helicopter?" I reply.

"No. Go find him. Now!"

~~
Chapter 21

~

Shawn

Shawn has never felt pain this intense. It's as if he's already dead and he's suffering some cruel form of eternal punishment. There's white-hot, searing pain running through his spine, and spreading to every single nerve in his body. He hears a piercing shriek rip through the air. He knows the person screaming must be him.

Suddenly, everything becomes numb. He can't feel anything, and somehow, he knows this is because the bones in his spine are all broken. After that, it's a strange mix of pain, kind of a searing, burning, numbing pain.

Shawn starts seeing spots, and almost instantly blacks out.

~

Emma

Meanwhile, Emma's on the third floor of Camp Takes. There's fire all around her, having recently taken the life of the tenth Transmorgifer. Now, she faces are two choices: She can either try to maneuver her way through the fire out of the building, possibly suffering major burns or even death. On the other hand, she can jump twenty-five feet to the ground, also possibly causing death.

She turns around and immediately, she knows her first option is out of the question. The fire is everywhere; there's no possible way to creep around it. It's quickly making its way towards her.

Emma turns around prepares herself to jump. She knows that this could be it, she could die from this. She slowly inhales a mix of oxygen and smoke, knowing this could be her last. A rush of adrenaline goes through her body, and then she's flying towards the ground. Her death could be coming closer and closer.

She's almost to the ground.

Her wrist hits the ground first, and then she can hear it shatter.

But then her head hits the ground, and she immediately goes unconscious.

~

Lucy

Lucy is on the helicopter. Four are missing. Her foot is in excruciating pain from her wound. Her ribs don't feel right, and she's sure they must be bruised from the fall that she and Sophia took.

Despite this, she's taken the initiative to help the plan succeed. She's done a headcount of the Transmorgifers, and nine out of thirteen of them are on here. The ex-campers are all knocked out on the ground, unconscious from exhaustion.

Of these four missing, three of them are the most important to the mission.

In moments, Lochbion's troops are storming the scene of the fire, trying to put it out, figure out what's going on, and why it even started.

"Crap. More people to brainwash," the pilot says, noticing the troops down below.

"Go!" The co-pilot of the helicopter tells the pilot as three bodies are lifted onto the helicopter. Lucy knows it's Shawn, Emma, and Sophia.

She hopes they're all right. As she sees their unconscious bodies, she knows that "all right" is simply impossible.

~

Sophia

Healing centers are now probably my least favorite place ever. Ever since my experience at Camp Takes, which looked like a healing center that destroyed instead of healed, I've always felt uncomfortable in them. So when I wake in a healing center, my first instinct is to scream and run. I look down at my right arm, and I see a tube leading into an IV.

My next instinct is to rip it out, but then I check the color of the liquid. It's clear. None of the sickly colors at Camp Takes. I still feel a bit sketchy about the IV.

A nurse comes striding in. "Ah, good. You're finally awake," she says.

"What . . . what happened to me?" I ask.

"Actually, you're pretty lucky. Your ankle was sprained, and your left hand got completely crushed by a huge piece of debris, shattering all the bones in it. It could have been a lot worse, with the circumstances you were in," she explains to me. I look at my left hand, and sure enough, it's in a healing tube that they use to mend broken bones. My elbow is attached to the side of the healing tube, holding up my arm so no pressure is put on my injured hand.

I look back up at the nurse. "What about Shawn, Emma, and Lucy? And the Transmorgifers we saved?" I ask.

The nurse's face tightens. "Apart from one of them dying from the flames at Camp Takes, all of the rescued Transmorgifers are fine. The ex-campers are currently being nursed back to health, because, as you know from personal experience, they've been used as test dummies for science and have been completely underfed during their experience at Camp Takes."

"Don't remind me," I groan, as I automatically start rubbing the white scars all over my body; it's the habit I've developed whenever somebody brings up that awful place.

"Well, Lucy didn't suffer any major injuries. You know, a bruised ribcage, and a nasty cut on her foot. She's going to be released today," the nurse tells me.

"You didn't say anything about Shawn or Emma," I tell her.

"Would you like to see them?"

"YES!" I shout. She quickly helps me into a wheelchair, since I can't stand up because of my sprained ankle. She disconnects the healing tube holding my hand from the bed, and attaches it to the wheelchair. She leads me out of the room, and into the winding hallways.

Although the nurse doesn't realize it, I'm internally screaming. Simply being in a wheelchair brings terrifying memories flooding back into my brain. *It's not Camp Takes. It's not Camp Takes. You're going to see Shawn and Emma. It's not Camp Takes. It's only the healing center somewhere in Prudence.*

Soon enough, she stops me in front of a room. "This is Emma's room," the nurse tells me.

"How is she?" I ask.

"She's got a broken wrist and three broken ribs."

"Is that all?"

"No. . ." She leads me into the room, but I'm not sure I want to see what's inside.

~

I was right. I don't want to see what's inside. Emma has a healing tube on her wrist, just like the one I have on my hand.

But the thing that shocks me the most is the healing chamber covering everything from her neck up.

Emma's eyes are shut tight, and she's obviously out cold.

"Why is there a healing chamber on her head?" I choke out, a combination of shrieking and coughing.

"She's got some major brain damage," Emma's nurse explains as he refills an IV going into her arm. "She fell from 25 feet up, and we're lucky she's not dead. Don't worry, we've healed most of it, but there's going to be some problems. She's going to have short-term memory and she's going to be blind in her right eye."

Short term memory,. Partial blindness. I let it soak in, but my mouth speaks before I can think, and I yell at the nurses. "You people are awful! You said we'd get out of there alive, and it looks like she's about to die!" I would be standing up and throwing a fit if I didn't have a sprained ankle and a hand trapped in this stupid healing tube.

"Be assured, Sophia, she only has a 2% chance of dying. Emma's going to be fine."

"Except for partial blindness and short-term memory!" I yell. "Just get me out of here. Show me Shawn."

There is a BLEEP-BUZZ-BLEEP, probably coming from a transmitter the nurse has. She picks it up, and holds it to her ear. She gasps. Her jaw drops. "I thought he was in the best healing chamber in the country!" she says into the transmitter

After a few more moments, she hangs up. She gulps and looks around nervously. "I'm sorry, Sophia, but we can't allow you to see your brother. There have been some certain complications that have just arisen."

"WHAT HAPPENED?" I yell, my voice cracking. If Shawn's condition is even a little bit worse than Emma's, I'm going to be irate.

"You-bring-me-to-my-brother-right-now-he's-the-only-family-I-have-because-my-parents-are-probably-dead-right-now-he-better-be-all-right!" I cram out into one breath.

The nurse groans.

"Were you specifically told not to let me see him?" I ask.

"N-

"THEN YOU LET ME SEE HIM!" I scream.

"We have to take you back to your room first," the nurse says, a concerned look on her face.

"How is he? Let me see him!" I say.

"We can't let you," the nurse says. "It's a very complicated matter." She wheels me off back to my room, leaving me in the most anxious state I've ever been in my entire life.

"What happened?" I ask as she sets me back into my bed, and hooks up the IV back up to my arm. "Tell me. Now."

The nurse is on the brim of tears. I know what she has to say must be awful. "Shawn's condition . . . is worse than

Emma's. His spine is fractured, and he's suffered the most severe burns we've ever seen," the nurse says.

"What . . . What's the percentage . . . of living?" I spit out. I try not to cry, but I can't stop it. My face is covered in tears already and there's nothing I can do about it. I'm hyperventilating, my palms are sweaty, and I'm completely overwhelmed. Now the nurse has tears streaming down her face as well. She's pressing a few buttons on the machine where my IV is hooked up to.

"The percentage of living," the nurse says, "Is . . . ten. Ten percent."

. . .

. . .

. . .

. . .

"TEN PERCENT?"

. . .

"What happened, and why does he have a ten percent chance of dying? Is he dead already?"

. . .

"I'm afraid you're going to need to rest now," the nurse says as she presses another button on the machine hooked up to my IV. I take this as code word for, "We're going to drug you asleep," even though she didn't directly say that.

"You'll be asleep before you can count to ten in your head," she smiles.

Try me. I think. *Okay, one, two, three, four . . .*

. . .

. . .

~

And then I'm awake again. I don't know how long it's been, but my hand has been removed from the healing tube. Now, there's a hard, clear cast on it. When I try moving my foot, my ankle doesn't hurt as much as I thought it would be. Either I've been out for a very long time or they've done something to help speed up the healing process.

The nurse from before is standing next to my IV machine, pressing more buttons. "We're giving you a calming drug." It takes me a moment to remember why, but then the terrible memories come flooding back. Shawn has a ten percent chance of living.

"Tell me what happened to Shawn," I order her. I want to feel angry and curse at her, but the calming drug enters my body and begins working its magic.

"He suffered major burns on one of his legs, and we had to take it off from the knee down. He'll be an amputee," she begins to explain. *Great. He has a ten percent chance of living and if he does, he won't have one of his legs. Just great.* I think there's anger rushing through my head, but the calming drug is canceling it out.

"Other than that, there were second and third degree burns scattered all around, covering almost all of his body. Some are worse than others, and some are healed, and others, well, will leave some huge scars. There was a huge chunk of debris from the building that landed and broke his spine and his ribs. He's going to be completely paralyzed as well," she explains.

"Right now," she gulps. "We've put him in a medically induced coma."

My eyes widen. *A coma?* I have the sudden urge to kick and punch something, anything, but it goes away as the relaxing medicine kicks in again. I must be pretty angry for me to override a strong calming drug. But I have a right to. This is my brother. Shawn. They said the mission would be a success, but I don't know how they could call it such with my brother in a coma.

I remember what the nurse said earlier over her transmitter. "I thought he was in 'the best healing chamber in the country,'" I tell her, making air quotes over the words 'best healing chamber in the country.'

"Oh, you must've heard my conversation," the nurse sighs, wiping a tear off her face. "He was, and still is, but we had to put him in a coma. He wasn't able to sleep because of the intense pain he was going through, and even our sleeping drugs and pain relief drugs wouldn't help. Please understand," she says, punching in more buttons, almost overdosing on this calming drug.

Suddenly, a strange rush of joy runs through my body as the nurse presses more buttons on my IV machine, shooting drugs into my body. This joy doesn't feel real. It feels artificial and fake, but I don't care. At least I get to let go of my worries, if only for a short time.

"Welcome to my invitation! What the Monday indigo?" I yell out, giggling. Something tells me I should be angry, but for some strange reason, I feel calm and silly. "Take turns looking! There's a train going by. Stop! We need an owl!"

As I start giggling about the strange things I'm saying, I remember in the back of my mind the nurse putting me on a calming drug, and it must be doing its job well. I'd rather be slap-happy than have to worry about Shawn.

Suddenly, Emma's nurse from before comes in again, and he smiles. "I have some good news for you,"

"Happy birthday!!!" I scream out, giggling. My nurse leans over and whispers something into his ear.

"Oh, okay," he says. "Sophia? Your friend, Emma, is conscious. She's out of her healing tube, and is going to be released in a few days," he says. "Would you like to see her?"

"If Emma's not okay, I'm going to come to your house in the middle of the night, slam your head into a refrigerator door, give you a root canal without the anesthetic, and mercilessly clobber you with a morbidly obese plush gorilla!" I yell out, a wave of laughs going through me.

That nurse looks like a penguin. I keep giggling as he unplugs the IV from my arm, lifts me onto a wheel chair, and rolls me out of the room.

"In fact," my nurse says, "we're releasing *you* today,"

"So this guy walks into a bar. Ouch," I snicker silently.

I keep rambling on with forced joy and silliness as we go down the hallway. "See, honey, we took out the Kevlar lining, which makes it much more slimming, but far less bulletproof," I tell Emma's nurse, who's pushing me down the hallway with a faint smile on his face. "But, we'll just have to make do! You'll be on the runway in five minutes! You look GORGUS!"

"What are you saying?" the nurse asks.

"It's a secret to everybody."

As we make our way to Emma's room, my silliness and giggles die down. The drug must be wearing off. As the emotional and physical pain settles back, I almost want to be loopy again. I'm almost back to normal as I enter Emma's room.

"Emma!" I call out to her as I'm wheeled over to where she's sitting.

"Sophia?" she asks. Her bright green eyes twinkle. I can't help but think that one of them is blind now.

"Yes, it's me!" I say, bending over to hug her gently. She's got a cast on her wrist, just like mine.

"I'm so glad we got out alive," she says. "What happened to me? I can't remember half of what went on there."

"Um, you kind of fell 25 feet and got, uh, brain damage," I say.

"So that must be why I can't see out of this eye," she says, pointing to her right eye. "But what's -" she asks, but stops mid-sentence. My hands tense. This must be the memory problems. It's as if she forgot she was saying something.

"Can I see Shawn?" she asks.

"Unfortunately, not yet, Emma," her nurse says. He stands up and leaves the room so Emma and I can be alone.

"Shawn," she says. "I remember him. I think he . . . I think he loves me." My stomach is churning, but I have to stay strong for Emma.

"Yes, Emma," I say, tears brimming at the edges of my eyes. "He does."

She looks down for a moment. "I think I love him," she whispers. "When can I see him?"

"Emma, did you know that Shawn. . ." I say, but I don't finish. Does she know he's in a coma?

"Can't he turn into an elephant?" she whispers. Her eyes look up quickly, looking into mine. "He's a Transmorgifer. And so are you. What's a Transmorgifer?"

Now I really want to scream. "You're a Transmorgifer too," I say to her.

I recall when Emma first explained what a Transmorgifer was to me. It's like that situation, only in reverse, as I explain how she's a Biomorph and Shawn and I are Aniversi.

"I remember that," she says. "I think."

Emma's nurse enters again. "Sophia, if you'd like, you can see Shawn now," he says.

"Why can't I see him?" Emma complains.

"You will," he says. "Soon."

"What's a Transmorgifer?" Emma asks as I am rolled out of her room. Shawn's room is only a few doors down, but the trip there seems to take forever. I know this could be completely dreadful.

~

But when I enter, it's not as bad as I expected. Shawn lies flat in one huge healing tube, surrounding his whole entire body. He's hooked up to way too many tubes to count, obviously checking his vital signs and helping him stay alive.

I can see that only one leg is peeking out from the gown he's wearing. *That's because they had to amputate it. It was burned so badly.* I wonder what it will be like if he survives, having to live as an amputee.

I want to hug him so badly, but the healing chamber blocks me from doing such. At least he's alive. *But he only has a ten percent chance of living.* No. But he's still alive.

And he's my brother. I know he can get through this.

~

Later in the day, the Embassy requests the appearance of Emma and me. Emma has shown up in a wheelchair, and I'm the last to enter the room. Lucy is there as well.

"Have a seat," Commander Carvenaw says. I take the only empty seat, the one right next to Emma's.

"What do you want?" I ask, words slipping out of my mouth before I can stop them. "It's all because of this stupid mission that Shawn's in a coma."

"And nine lives were saved from being lab rats, all of the files stored in Camp Takes' data system deleted, and the building itself burned to the ground. Camp Takes is no more, and if they try to start up something new, they won't have anybody to test on. We've checked the current records, and there aren't any Transmorgifers living in Lochbion at the current time," he says.

"But Shawn. . ."

"But Sophia," Lucy cuts in," We helped out all of these people."

"So, we have thirteen Transmorgifers to take care of now. One of them is currently in a coma, so what are we going to do with the other twelve?" one of the Embassy members says.

"Well, what are you going to do with us?" I ask.

"Give you a place where all Transmorgifers can be safe and learn how to use their powers wisely," says Commander Carvenaw.

"Ivandale Hall?" I ask.

"No," he says.

"Then where will we go?"

"We have an idea," says one of the Embassy members. "We would just like to run it past you three."

"You will live with the other saved Transmorgifers in an abandoned inn we've found on the outskirts of Prudence. It'll be called the Glass Hotel. You'll also have the opportunity to go to school here in town, and in you spare time, learn how to use their powers to good use."

"Who's going to teach them?" I ask.

"Why, you. And Lucy. And possibly Emma," Commander Carvenaw says.

"Emma likes that idea," Emma says. I don't think she realizes she's talking in third person.

"All of the Transmorgifers that have been saved have been released today. Sophia, Lucy, if you'd like, you can go ahead and go there now, if you'd like," Commander Carvenaw tells us.

"Wait, aren't I supposed to be at Ivandale Hall?" Lucy asks. "I still have four years of training left."

"Do you want to go back to Ivandale Hall?" he asks her.

ANIVERSI

"Well, not exactly," Lucy says, looking down. "I guess I wasn't really made to be an agent for Terranary."

"That's all right. We'll sort things out with your father, and you can help Sophia and Emma out," he explains.

"Really?" Lucy asks. Commander Carvenaw nods.

"Emma, I'm afraid that you haven't officially been released yet. You can meet up with Sophia and Lucy in a few days when that happens," Commander Carvenaw says. Emma nods.

"Sophia? Lucy? How about you two go ahead to the Glass Hotel. The other Transmorgifers will meet you there shortly."

~

When Commander Carvenaw said "Glass Hotel", I was expecting a hotel of glass. It surprises me when I see an old building with cracked and chipped paint and rusty metal. It's located in outer Prudence, and it isn't that busy around. Few people are walking the sidewalks near us.

Hmm. This isn't really glass. But then again, I think the glass part of the name is signifying the code for Transmorgifers being safe.

"I think it's perfect," Lucy says, gazing at the building. She looks at me. "Don't tell my dad, but I'd rather stay here than Ivandale. I guess that wasn't really my thing."

"I won't tell him," I smile. "Let's go in."

And so Lucy and I approach the building. The rusted door makes a loud CREAK! when we open it.

Inside the building, there is a tiny lobby. To our left is a wooden desk with some old papers scattered around it. Next to the desk, there are a few couches in an ugly yellow shade. Directly next to the lobby is a room that obviously used to be a breakfast area. There's five tables scattered around and about, with some twenty chairs. Great. Even more than we'll need.

The government's going to provide our food. You can't really expect a bunch of adolescent Transmorgifers to get jobs *and* help teach new students.

I begin to explore the downstairs with Lucy. Along with the dining room, there are five large meeting rooms. These will be perfect for training sessions. At the end of the hall, there's an elevator to a second floor. I walk over to the brass doors and press the button next to them. I wonder if it's still working, despite the age of this building.

Sure enough, the elevator makes a BING! sound and it opens. I walk inside. There's two buttons, one that says "G," probably standing for "Ground." Along with that, there's a "1." I press the button that has the 1 on it. There are probably bedrooms on this floor. The elevator creaks up one story.

When it opens, I can see there are about twenty doors leading into rooms. Ten on one side of the hall, and ten on the other. I start walking down one of the hallways, and I open the door and enter. It's smaller than my room at Ivandale, but larger than my room back at school.

There's a single double-sized bed, a small bathroom with a sink and a shower. Along with this, there's a window at the end of the room.

Or, well, what used to be a window. It's been broken, and there are shards of glass all over the floor. I step towards them, making sure not to step on them.

I pick one of the shards up, being careful not to touch the edges. I look at my reflection in it. I can't tell how it's been broken. Was it hit by something? Did it shatter simply because it's incredibly old?

Or was it intentional? Could this be a message from the Embassy?

I don't care whether the shard of glass was intentional or not, I just hope it means what the shard-of-glass code intends: I am safe here.

Acknowledgements

While I would love to elaborate on how amazing all of these people are, there are so many people, it'd take another novel to explain how amazing these people are.

This book would not have been possible without the following people:

My lord and savior Jesus Christ, who gave me strength and courage to do this project. Without him, I would be nowhere. He loves me no matter what I do, and he will always be there to welcome me home.

My family, who listens to countless ramblings on stupid stuff about books and writing and whatnot, and has to deal with my writing comas and the fact I'd rather write a book than play cards.

My other family, including Eli, Abby, Clayton, Eden, Jerry, Katie, Ashley, Jamie, and Rachel. You guys are amazing.

Maddie, because she kept me going even though I was about ready to quit this project. Without her amazing feedback, you wouldn't be reading this.

Taylor, for being a freaking awesome beta reader. He helped me realize that this story isn't a completely stupid and childish idea. BTW, in that last chapter, where Sophia is loopy, half the things she said I've stolen from him. (Don't ask about the morbidly obese plush gorilla . . .) *Grammar Police High Five*

And last, but certainly not least, my best friend in the whole world, Grace Smith. She was the first one to hear this crazy idea I had where three teenagers escaped a futuristic country. She is, and will always be, my favorite fangirling, writing, reading, book nerd, cheez-it loving, prosecuting, Mexican Squid drawing, Leo obsessed, amazing fantastilastical friend.

ANIVERSI

Pronunciations:

Aniversi: Ann-ih-verse-eye

Transmorgifer: trans-morg-ih-pher

Biomorph: Bye-oh-morph

Chlorophist: kloro-fist

Planecopter: Pl-ayne-ih-cop-terr

About the Author

Aniversi is Hannah Phipps' debut novel. She is fourteen years old and lives in the United States. She has been writing ever since she was seven and her mother showed her the word processor. In her spare time, Hannah loves to perform onstage with her theatre group, play video games on her Wii or Gamecube, or sit down and read a good book. She hopes to write more books in her future.